DAUGHTER OF THE PLAIN FOLK

by

S. EARL DUBBEL

MOODY PRESS

CHICAGO

To

Kristin, Kari, and Ingrid, and Grandmother Dubbel,
with love from Granddaddy

Library of Congress Catalog Card Number: 72-95023

ISBN: 0-8024-1761-2

Printed in the United States of America

Contents

1

New Privilege

WHEN BETSY BRECHER was twelve years old, in August 1894, she was permitted for the first time to sit on the last row with the other girls in the meetinghouse of the Old Order Dunkers in southern Pennsylvania. This was a glowing experience for her, like being promoted in school, and she felt she was quite grown up now. The last row in the rear of the large section occupied by the sisters was reserved for the girls of the Old Order families, who had not yet joined the church.

During the morning service of three sermons interspersed by two rather long prayers, Betsy's childish enthusiasm began to taper off; and she thought more seriously of all that this new privilege implied. Next she must join the church and become a sister.

Oh, if only Papa would be satisfied to let me stay here with the girls for a while!

Becoming a sister in one of the Old Order Dunker congregations would make Betsy an official member of a group which strictly practiced the simple form of worship and the plain mode of life of their ancestors and frowned upon any change as "worldly." It would mean steadfast, unwavering loyalty to the church and close friendships only with other Old Order Dunkers.

Betsy wondered what it would be like to grow up and

always live that way, while all about them new inventions and scientific marvels promised to make the oncoming twentieth century an exciting time to live in. New ideas and doubts had begun to nag persistently in her mind lately.

I'm not sure I feel quite ready to be a sister.

She absentmindedly flipped the cover of her hymnbook and jostled the elbow of her cousin, Ann, who glanced at her disapprovingly.

Betsy thought of the many times she had sat beside her mother in the midst of the other sisters. Her three brothers still sat there: Jakie, age eight; Johnny, age six; and Amos, age five. They sat quietly, as Betsy also had always done. She sat up primly in her new seat and tried to be more intent on doing just the right thing so that this new privilege might not be taken from her.

However, after two hours of the service, Elder Kurtz got up to preach the final sermon; and Betsy could not help yawning. Then she yawned again.

Ann frowned at her and whispered, "What makes you so fidgety?"

Betsy just shrugged and smiled meekly.

Up until she was twelve, Betsy always had enjoyed going to meeting and assumed that the Old Order was unquestionably the best of all churches. She had felt at home in the Old Order service and learned to pay attention to the three or four sermons each Sunday morning. She especially enjoyed the sermons of her father, Elder Jacob Brecher. She thought he was the finest looking of all the elders and certainly the best preacher. It was easy to remember the points of his sermons because he often used illustrations drawn from his farm work and talked about his sermons with the family as they rode home after the service. Her mother had a lovely voice, and Betsy would follow her in singing the hymns, blending her voice in sweetly. The feeling of family unity was even more strong when her father did the "lining"—the reading by an elder of each line before it was sung, according to the ancient custom from the days before they had printed hymnals. Even though the members now had hymnbooks, lining the hymns had become a cherished custom and was not to be abandoned!

Betsy glanced at the sisters seated before her, row upon row, all dressed alike in their dark-gray, floor-length dresses and white prayer caps. She recalled hearing a prominent lady in town say to her mother, "Laura and Betsy are just too pretty to be penned up for life in those ugly Dunker dresses!"

For life! Betsy felt confused and dismayed. Becoming a sister had to be considered very seriously. She knew she was not ready to make such an important decision.

After the Presiding Elder Mitchell gave the closing prayer of the two-and-a half-hour service, the members greeted each other, according to the Scripture, "with a holy kiss." The sisters kissed the other sisters who sat near them, and the brethren, who sat in the large section across the main aisle, kissed each other. For the first time in her life, Betsy looked upon this scene with some uncertainty of mind.

As the Brecher family drove the twelve miles home in their horse-drawn carriage, Betsy and Laura sat in the front seat with their father, and the three boys rode in the rear with their mother. Elder Brecher talked to his daughters about the service, explaining various points of the sermons. He noticed that his younger daughter was unusually quiet.

"Well, Betsy, how do you like sitting with the other girls? You must feel very grown up." He smiled at her affectionately.

"Yes, Papa, it was very nice." Betsy's eyes remained on the neatly plowed fields they were passing.

"Sitting in the last row is just a step in the direction of joining the sisterhood," Papa declared solemnly. "I want you to think and pray about joining the church very soon."

Betsy squirmed and her face became red. Her father sounded as though he already had made up her mind for her.

Oh, if only I could talk with Papa alone about this.

When they reached home, Betsy ran up the stairs to the room that she shared with Laura. Just then she heard her father coming up the stairs. She asked him to come into her room.

"Dear Papa," she began, looking so earnest, "I shall always be glad to attend meeting with you and the family, yet I wish you would let me wait until I can feel more sure about joining the Old Order."

Her father was silent for a while, then he said, "Betsy, you know what I want you to do. It is an important matter which you must pray about." When he left the room, she threw herself onto her bed and cried. She was sure that her father would not relent.

Now in his forties, Elder Brecher was the sort of man who found satisfaction in his family and in having amicable relations with the members of the congregation. Although he loved all his children, he seemed somewhat partial to Betsy, who seemed always cheerful and eager to please others. Laura, the eldest, was an attractive girl too, but she tended to be willful and bossy with the younger ones. Elder Brecher declared that nobody could enjoy home and church more than he, and he couldn't imagine anything happening to mar his happy family life. He felt sorry for people who missed the joy and contentment that belonging to the Old Order provides.

There was never any question about Betsy's fondness for her Old Order home life. The most outstanding characteristic of this home was its even tenor. Changes came only with the orderly procession of the seasons, which signalled different occupations in both house and field. Betsy early learned to look forward to each season's highlights: housecleaning, plowing, and sowing in the spring; berry picking, haying, and cultivating in the summer; harvesting, preserving, and butchering in the autumn; baking, sewing, and sleigh riding in the winter.

When Betsy was six, the long-looked-for start to school

actually occurred. The school was in a boxlike frame building containing two large rooms, about a mile from her home.

In spite of its simplicity, school was a new world for Betsy. She was keen in observing everything but was puzzled by the interests of the other children. Some of the girls wore their hair so differently from her neat, shiny braid; and she noticed several of the girls wearing rings. This puzzled her at first, but she thought the rings were so pretty. What astonished her was to hear the girls talking during recess about birthday parties they had enjoyed. She asked her mother what this meant but her mother only said, "We don't believe in doing such things."

There were some girls in her room who came from other Old Order families: Samantha Reddig, a distant cousin, and Sarah and Rebecca Kimler, whom Betsy had known at church ever since she was two years old. But from the first Betsy liked Jenny Howe and Thelma Price and several others who belonged to a group of girls from what she had heard called the worldly churches. When Samantha Reddig saw Betsy playing with them, she told her she must play at recess only with "our people." When Betsy persisted in playing with the other girls, Samantha and Sarah and Rebecca glared at her angrily.

"You're a worldly body!" yelled Samantha.

Betsy stopped running. "Why do you say such a thing, Samantha?"

Samantha stuck out her tongue at her. "Because it's true! My papa says your papa is a worldly man. Just see how proud he is, the way he cuts and brushes his hair! And you're worldly too. Just see how proud you are! You want to be with the fancy people, and you're being downright untrue to the Old Order."

Jenny Howe scowled. "Don't pay attention to her, Betsy. She's always saying ugly things!"

One day Miss Stoner, the teacher, had to caution Betsy about talking to a child at an adjoining desk; and later out on the playground, Betsy joked that Miss Stoner had big ears. Samantha ran to tell the teacher that Betsy was talking about her out on the playground and saying mean things.

When the teacher had heard Betsy's explanation, she smiled. "We'll just forget about it."

"How can I forget?" asked Betsy. "Samantha seems to want to cause trouble for me. But I will be nice to her anyway."

Miss Stoner smiled kindly. "I see, Betsy, that you have a problem, but the best way to handle it is to forgive, and to be pleasant and friendly to all the girls. Then you will truly be a practicing Christian."

Betsy often thought about that. She liked the idea that she could be a "practicing Christian," even though she was not yet a member of the Old Order church. She admired her pleasant and attentive teacher, and dreamed of what it would be like someday to be a teacher "just like Miss Stoner."

After school, Betsy and Laura would hurry home to finish their chores and then run to play. Sometimes they went up to Uncle John's farm to play with cousin Ann.

When the boys were at hand, along with Silas Butterbaugh from another Old Order family, the children sometimes played church. Silas and Jakie and Johnny would represent the elders and the girls were the sisters. Each girl would place a handkerchief on her head to represent the little white prayer cap. "Elder" Silas or "Elder" Jacob would recite each line of a hymn, then all would sing just as they did at meeting.

What Betsy enjoyed most as she was growing older, was having company at home for dinner. Nothing could be more pleasant than when the dinner table, made up of two cherry drop-leaf tables joined together, was surrounded by the Macks and the Stovers after the Sunday morning service. The six children of the Stover family, the two children of the Mack family, and the three Brecher boys were careful not to fidget as they sat with their fathers. The wives waited on the table, serving roast duck with mashed and scalloped potatoes, fresh vegetables in season, hot bread, and many sorts of pickles and preserves. For dessert, the women served a large helping of apple pie and cream pie to each one.

During the meal, Elder Brecher interested everyone by telling about a visit Friday evening at the offices in town of the hustling young business man, Nick Mellers. "His burly father was storming about three of his grandsons at his home who had rushed in one evening after a ball game, furiously arguing about it. When he tried to quiet them, they became even more boisterous and rushed from the home, shouting at each other. The grandfather turned to me, as I stood just inside the door, and said with emphasis, 'Why, Jake, I'm telling you what you know already, but I want you to know I know it. The Old Order home is the last vestige in America of the old-fashioned, peaceful home, with order maintained by the head of the house!'

" 'Good, why don't you and your family join with us?' I suggested. But he explained that they were committed elsewhere. 'But I'm telling you, I have powerful respect for you plain folk. Yes, sir,' he insisted, 'the last vestige of quiet, peaceful homelife!'

"Well, we ought to be glad we have such happy homes," Elder Brecher finished, with a pleased expression.

Everyone at the table wanted to take part in the conversation, expressing pride and satisfaction in being Old Order, and gratitude for what the church handed down to them. Betsy's mother mentioned that there recently had been an incident at school when Betsy was asked to explain about the Old Order. Mrs. Brecher asked Betsy to tell the company of her experience.

As she had been trained not to speak until her elders had first spoken to her, Betsy was pleased to tell her story. In speaking to her class, she related what she had heard her father say were essential characteristics of the Old Order home, such as the members working to maintain a home life with peace and quiet, and the value placed upon work as

---

good for the soul. Each family member has his work to do and enjoys doing it. When his work is done, he is free to do whatever interests him. Frugality is also an essential, for it is a sin to be wasteful; and she quoted the saying, "Willful waste makes woeful want." Betsy mentioned also the belief in the sanctity of a promise, and the aim to develop in the young a loyalty to one's family. Finally she mentioned her father's explanation that the Old Order Dunkers take a middle position between extremes found among the plain folk, such as to require only those who have joined the church to wear the plain garb instead of requiring all the children to wear it regardless of age or their having joined the church.

The guests around the dinner table declared that Betsy had done better than any of them could have done. Her father said he was happy over her being such a good witness of the Old Order practices, and her face beamed.

Betsy was eager to learn at home as well as at school. As her mother was the seamstress for the family, she made the dresses for herself and both the girls. Betsy learned to sew and knit, and was an apt pupil. She thought knitting was as entertaining as any sort of play; and during the hard winter when she was twelve, she knitted sweaters for each member of the family. She thought cooking was good fun too and was eager to help her mother with dinner so she might learn from her. More than anything, she wanted to make cream pies, fruit pies, and shoo-fly pies as well as her mother, for they were the most delicious treats she could imagine.

When Betsy entered high school in Waynesboro, she joined Laura in walking almost three miles to town every day, except when the weather was bad, and then her father hitched horse and buggy to drive them to town. The long walk helped them to become strong and robust with ruddy cheeks and agile bodies.

Both girls did well in school. Laura excelled in doing written compositions, and she declared that after she finished high school she wanted to work in the office of the local evening newspaper. She graduated from high school while Betsy was a sophomore. That same year Laura realized her ambition with a job in the office of the *Blue Ridge Zephyr* of Waynesboro, which had a large circulation in this town of several thousand people, almost three miles from her home.

Betsy was eager to learn. Now she was discovering so many new things that made life seem exciting, and her studies of history and literature raised so many interesting questions that she thought learning the most fascinating thing in the world. Along with her knowledge of the world beyond her immediate vicinity grew her doubts and resistance to joining the Old Order sisterhood.

2

Questionings

ELDER BRECHER had begun at the age of twenty-one to make his living on the farm he inherited from his father. Each year he managed to save money and soon was able to buy rundown farms at sheriff's sales. He worked hard to restore them, then sold them at a substantial profit. He was careful to invest his earnings in the thriving industries in town which had been started by men of the community, some of whom were Old Order; and he became in time a substantial stockholder.

Although he was reticent about his financial success and continued to practice the thrift and industry he had learned in his boyhood home, it somehow began to circulate throughout the Shady Gap congregation that he had become a man of means. Some of the members apparently resented his success and became captious, complaining especially about his older children—that Laura missed the Sunday morning service too often, and Betsy was too much occupied with outside activities at high school, such as singing in the chorus.

This was the first vexing problem in Betsy's high school life. The instructor in music noticed that she had a pleasing soprano voice and encouraged her to join the chorus. She attended the first rehearsal and enjoyed it so much that she told the director she would be very happy to be a member if her parents permitted it. When she told her parents, her

14

mother expressed interest, and her father remarked that doing this would be irregular for a child of the Old Order but didn't say no absolutely. She felt she had their approval and began to attend, never missing a rehearsal. The lovely semiclassical music fascinated her, and only when she was at church on Sunday did she wonder whether it might be worldly to sing such songs.

But there was another inducement to belong to the chorus, besides her enjoyment of the music. Another chorus member, Doris Karl, who sang soprano and came from a cultivated home in town, took a fancy to Betsy. Betsy liked her too, and a close friendship began. Doris invited Betsy to her home for dinner, and Betsy experienced more of the world than she ever had before. When she walked into the living room and stood before one of the pictures, a reproduction of Constable's *Cornfield,* she was almost cast under a spell by the beauty of the picture. She noticed everything—the ripening grain, the trees, the boy drinking from the brook as he stretched out on the ground. She couldn't take her eyes off the picture. "Oh," she exclaimed to Doris, "you know, we aren't allowed to have any pictures on the wall, almost nothing at all. But this is lovely!" She looked at the other pictures and was fascinated by the picture of a forest which she learned was by Ruysdael.

Betsy's spirit seemed to catch fire from her enjoyment of these pictures. She became more aware of beauty around her, as on the next afternoon, when she was walking down from Uncle John's farm to her home, she was struck by the beauty of the sunset. It had been a cloudy day, but suddenly the sun blazed forth, coloring a myriad of clouds with a smoky gold. Instinctively she responded to the beautiful—in nature and in manmade objects. She noticed the dresses Doris and her mother wore, their jewelry and the styles of their hair. Often now, as she walked home from Doris's house, she asked herself if she could feel satisfied with the plain simplicity of the Old Order.

Once when Betsy's father was absent from home, she was permitted by her mother to go with the Karl family over to Chambersburg one evening to enjoy a piano recital in which Doris's older sister, Virginia, was to participate. Betsy was so impressed that she thought nothing could be lovelier than that wonderful piano music!

As Betsy and Laura advanced in their teen years, Elder Brecher became more and more concerned that his daughters join the church. He often spoke earnestly to them, and their obvious reluctance and delay grieved him deeply. He and his family before him had been richly blessed by their Old Order ways, and he wanted his children to have such blessings also.

One Sunday morning Betsy and Laura were listening attentively to a sermon by their father after three other sermons had been preached. He had waxed eloquent in his sermon in the crowded meetinghouse, his face flushed as he pounded the table in front of him and stressed that the children of Old Order families should join the church in their early teens. Betsy's face became pale as she looked over at Laura to see if she too were disturbed, but Laura merely raised her eyebrows quizzically and shrugged her shoulders as if to say why be disturbed?

At the close of the sermon Betsy whispered, "Now Papa will be determined that we join!"

Many must have thought, *What about his own daughters?* Although the Old Order people do no proselytizing outside the fold, they cling with unceasing tenacity to the children of their own families.

While driving home, he talked to the girls very seriously about joining the church and revealed there had been complaints about his family from certain members, which the presiding elder had not discouraged.

Betsy woefully gazed at sunlit fields of gay spring flowers as she answered, "But really, Papa, I get a sort of chill whenever I think of having to give up wearing the dress I now wear and put on the plain garb."

"Ah, Betsy dear," said her father, gently pleading, "that won't be hard to do, for when you are baptized, your heart is changed and you will then want to be different from the world."

"But, Papa, if I were to wear the plain garb, I couldn't feel comfortable with my friends in town, because of the difference between us."

"Betsy," her father's voice deepened, "the important thing is to be loyal to your family church. And you should not have the kind of friends who'd make you feel uncomfortable wearing the plain garb."

"Papa, I'd feel uncomfortable even if I didn't have any friends in town. It's the utter lack of beauty a young girl feels in wearing such an unbecoming dress."

"Betsy, must I remind you again to pray for divine guidance! Remember, the Bible says, 'Lean not unto thine own understanding. In all thy ways acknowledge Him, and He shall direct thy paths.'"

"Papa, I have prayed for guidance, and still I can't feel right about wearing the plain garb."

"But, Betsy, in your praying you should be willing to have your mind changed."

Elder Brecher turned to Laura. "And my eldest should have made her decision long ago!"

Laura, now eighteen and graduated from high school, had admitted to Betsy that she hoped she could remain outside the Old Order. But she hedged, fearful of her father's reprimand. "Papa, I'd have to think a good deal more about such an important step before making a decision."

"Well now, girls, it isn't good to do so much thinking when action is called for!" replied their father in a firm but kindly tone. "I want you both to decide to join without further delay."

That afternoon after the dinner dishes were washed and

put away, Betsy for the first time in her life couldn't bring
herself to be interested in anything. The renewed concern of
her father that she join the Old Order church seemed like a
threat held over her. Her own home this afternoon didn't
seem as inviting as it always had before, and she pictured
instead Doris's lovely home in town where she had spent
the previous Sunday while Elder Brecher was conducting a
series of meetings in Virginia. She recalled how she had responded eagerly that morning to the Presbyterian service and
wondered if the sermon based on the text, "All things are
yours," taken from 1 Corinthians 3:21, was not meant especially for her! When they came home from church, Doris
played the piano and entertained Betsy with some songs by
Schubert. But her pleasure was marred by a feeling of guilt,
knowing that she should not have listened. She enjoyed looking again at the lovely pictures on the wall. She couldn't help
feeling what a pity it was the Old Order people were denied
so many things that were really beautiful.

Now as her gloom increased this Sunday afternoon, she
pictured herself dressed in the dark-gray calico floor-length
dress with its little matching shawl. If she became a sister,
she would wear a white prayer cap on her head; and whenever she went out, she would have to wear a black bonnet
with a tiny brim in the front. Then in her daydreams, she
imagined what it would be like to be Doris and wear the
pretty white dress her mother just bought for her.

Oh, she exclaimed to herself, *I don't want to look so ugly!*

She wondered if there was anything she could do to postpone the fateful day! If only she might continue to attend
the Old Order meeting and yet not become a member! She
recalled the talks about joining the church she had had with
her father during the past two years. She recognized that he
had not been harsh even though he was zealous. He admitted he was disappointed in her attitude and hoped she
soon would see the light.

Late that afternoon when her mother noticed that Betsy

had no appetite for supper and wondered what was wrong, Betsy confided, "I'm worried almost sick over Papa's wanting me to join the church."

"It is always difficult to make an important decision, dear." Mother spoke comfortingly. "But once you do and are baptized, you will be happier than ever before."

"Oh, no, Mamma dear, I'm not ready to take that step."

"Betsy, you've worried so much about joining the church that you're unable to see the benefits of being a sister in the Old Order."

"It's hard to be interested in the Old Order way of life after visiting Doris and enjoying the Presbyterian service so much," she confessed.

"Ach, yes, Betsy," her mother lamented, "I feared I was making a mistake to allow you to visit with Doris on Sunday."

"Oh no, Mamma, please don't think that was a mistake. Doris is a most helpful friend and so very sensible, and she's really a true Christian."

Ever since Betsy was a very young child, she had asked questions about the Old Order; and her father diligently related to her the history of the church. It was founded by a group of godly Germans at the beginning of the eighteenth century who under the influence of Pietism aimed at living an unworldly life. When they suffered persecution in Germany, William Penn welcomed them to Pennsylvania, and the steady growth of the denomination caused it to spread out into Maryland and Virginia and on into the Middle West. The denomination espoused no creed but what the Brethren found to be the plain teaching of the Bible. They were like the Quakers in refusing to bear arms in warfare. They stressed the wearing of the plain garb by both the men and the women, thereby indicating their separateness from the world. The men wore plain black hats and plain black coats without lapels, resembling a clergyman's coat. They wore no neckties. The women always wore white prayer caps, little shawllike coverings were their coats, and the black bonnet took the place of a hat.

Betsy learned from her father that their family had been members of the German Baptist Brethren from the beginning but had sided with the Old Order when a schism occurred in the 1880s between that conservative branch, who maintained resolutely the rigid customs and practices of the founding fathers, and the progressive group who tried to adjust their practice of the gospel to the changing conditions of the world. The progressive group, for instance, were not opposed to sending their children to college and, in fact, established a number of church-related colleges. Also they began to modify the traditional practice of wearing the plain garb.

The Old Order, on the other hand, concentrated on family life, especially in rural areas. The men were all hard workers on their farms, heeding the Old Testament dictum to "do with thy might what thy hands find to do." For a farmer to be prosperous was a sign that he was blessed of the Lord!

Betsy could see that it was a thriving church by the throngs of members who each year attended the annual meeting and by the large attendance of the members at their Sunday morning service. But she felt sorry for herself because the Old Order deprived her home of having any culture and beauty. A course at high school in civic government stressed how important it was for a citizen to be conscientious as a voter, and yet the plain folk forbid their members to vote! These seeming deprivations and civil abstentions rankled Betsy's sensitivity to beauty and thirst for knowledge.

At the high school she sought answers from a sympathetic instructor in English who had some relatives among the plain folk. This instructor appreciated Betsy's agile mind and liked to discuss problems with her after class. He tried to reconcile to her the age-old view of the plain folk that in order to fully worship and serve God one must not enjoy what the world enjoys. Hence they regarded worldliness today with the same abhorrence felt by the founders of the denomination at the beginning of the eighteenth century. Betsy was impressed to hear him add that "in some respects the Old Order Dunkers and the Mennonites represent the last stronghold in our country of the old-fashioned home with its peace and quiet." She was especially interested in his explanation that the tunes used in the Old Order Dunker hymns are the same as those used in the beginning of the eighteenth century, which were derived originally from the hymns of the Mennonites and have been traced even farther back to the Gregorian chant.

But her personal conflicts were not resolved.

With deepening concern and insistence, Elder Brecher talked to Betsy about the Old Order. Still unable to come to a decision, she took courage to say she would really like to know more about how some of the other churches worshiped God.

"Ach, Betsy," her father spoke sadly, "do you mean to say that after attending Old Order meeting all these years, you would be willing to abandon it and your family, and follow worldly customs?"

"Well, Papa, I am frank to tell you I really don't like the idea of being so entirely different from everybody else."

A frown replaced her father's kindly expression. Heavyheartedly he said he was grieved to find so much rebellion in his family and advised her again to pray more earnestly about her problem.

When Betsy was alone, she realized that her father's kind manner in dealing candidly with her made it all the more difficult for her to go counter to him. She was impressed by what her mother had said one day, that if she rebelled against her father in refusing to join the church, she might someday suffer a bad conscience over it. She did heed the advice of her parents and prayed often about her problem. She never failed to attend meeting with them or to participate in singing the hymns, which now seemed more interesting to her because of their ancient origin.

3

The Elders' Complaint

THERE WERE RUMBLINGS of dissatisfaction and open complaints shortly after Betsy began her senior year in high school. Members of the Shady Gap congregation were shocked to see a picture of Betsy Brecher, the daughter of an elder, in the town paper. The newspaper said she was popular with all the students and had been chosen as secretary of her senior class. But the church members thought it was scandalous that the daughter of an Old Order family should ever have her picture appear in the public press, for according to tradition, no member should ever have his picture taken. Many complained that Elder Brecher was too lenient with his family.

Early in October Betsy came home overjoyed at having been chosen to sing a solo in the cantata to be given by the high school chorus. As she walked home, she was too happy to give any thought to whether it was proper for her to be so enthusiastic. Being chosen today to sing a solo seemed to be the most wonderful thing that could happen. It was like being blessed by a fairy godmother whom she had read about in school. But she did begin to wonder what her father might say after he objected to her picture in the local paper. What if her picture appeared in the paper again? *My, oh my!* she mused. *What can be so dreadful about having one's picture in the paper?*

Betsy was later than usual in coming home that afternoon and hurried up the lane to give the news to her parents. Her father, who sat in his ladder-back rocking chair in the kitchen, looked up from the evening paper, smiling a little at her excitement.

"Oh," exclaimed Betsy, slightly out of breath. "I had to stay after the rehearsal to practice a solo that was just assigned to me."

Her father pulled at his long beard. "Ach, no, Betsy, you don't mean you got into another extra at school! That sounds like just too much!"

But her mother, who was working at the stove, turned around to remark, "It will help make her senior year good for her learning."

"It may be good for her learning, but it will be very difficult to explain to the other church elders," her father muttered. But then he resumed reading his paper.

The kitchen, a large square room in the rear of the house, reflected the plain philosophy of the Old Order. It served as a family room and a dining room as well. In the center stood a cherry drop-leaf table which served as the dining table. On it stood a large kerosene lamp. Elder Brecher sat in his roomy rocking chair beside the table. In one corner stood a large, walnut corner cupboard that he had made. A couch was on one side, and a window on the other. Spindle-back, plank-bottom chairs stood along the wall. On the walls there were no pictures, except that on a calendar from the bank in town showing a picture of a meadow in springtime, full of wild flowers. Next to the door was a sink with no running water, but a cistern was outside the door. The wood-burning kitchen range was near the sink. The wood box beside the stove was piled with split logs brought in each day by the boys.

Betsy now attended to her usual chores. As she ran to the

barn to collect the eggs, she thought of the difference between the life she was being reared in and the life of her school
mates—a difference of almost two hundred years, she guessed.
She reflected that when some of the children of the plain
folk come in contact with the ideas and practices of today,
they realize that they prefer the Old Order customs and join
the church and are satisfied, just as her mother must have
done. But she could foresee difficulty ahead for those who
were impressed with what the twentieth century soon would
have to offer. She thought of her Uncle John's brother, Zeke,
who drifted away from the church and became well-to-do in
his hardware store in town—and who, her mother had remarked, had had a difficult time with his family. Betsy knew
of the trouble her cousin Sally had when she didn't want to
join the Old Order church, and she shuddered to recall how
severe Aunt Mattie had been with her daughter until she became a sister.

Betsy appreciated that her father and mother were kind
and gentle, and she didn't like to think of the stark possibility
of any conflict with them. As she came back to the house
carrying the basket of eggs, she realized she always had enjoyed a happy relationship with her father, though of late it
seemed to her he was becoming unusually strict. She could
not forget her father's fear that the young people of the family might become unequally yoked with people of the world.

From her earliest years Betsy had looked up to her father
with admiration and trust. As a very little girl, she admired
his handsome head of thick, brown hair that he brushed
straight back, and his long, brown beard that tapered to a
point. His fondness for his little girl sometimes got the
better of his judgment, such as the time when she was five
and he playfully permitted her to sit on his lap with a pair
of scissors, trying to trim his beard. In the nick of time her
mother had intervened to keep the beard from becoming ir-
reparably lopsided! It seemed only a short time ago that she
had followed him so lovingly, wherever he might go or stand.

"God reward you, Betsy dear, for the joy I've always had in you," he frequently whispered.

As supper began that evening, there was no sign of tension but only happy fellowship in the Brecher home. Elder Brecher gave thanks for the food in his dignified way and closed by praying that "we all might rejoice in Thee." He asked each child to tell of highlights in the day.

Betsy told of her study of literature at school, how splendid her teacher was, and that she was now enjoying Addison's *Spectator Papers*. She talked of her girl friends at school and described Doris Karl's lovely home. "They have a maid to clean and to wait on the table and also a cook. But her parents want Doris to learn to cook. Her mother told me that Doris made a delicious corn pudding for dinner one evening, and every bit of it was eaten."

"Yes, Betsy," remarked her father, "their home may be very nice, but you want to remember that our family has been called to live according to our church and not like the world says."

"But, Papa, they are Christians. Mr. Karl says grace at meals just like you do, and Doris told me her father is an elder in the Presbyterian church."

Betsy continued, "After school today I talked with Mrs. Beinbrecht. She belongs to what she calls the Assembly. She gave me some more tracts after she learned I had read the ones she gave me weeks ago. She looked so concerned when she said she hoped I would remember we are not saved by our good works but only by trusting in what Christ has done for us."

This seemed to arouse her father. "Yes, of course, we recognize that God's grace is available for all believers because 'Christ died for our sins, according to the Scripture,' but He expects us to be active in good works, 'steadfast, always abounding in the work of the Lord.' That's why our church puts stress on good works."

"But, Papa, Mrs. Beinbrecht wouldn't disagree with that,

for she said that, when we believe and accept the Saviour, then we are to 'walk worthily of the high vocation wherewith we are called.' "

"Yes, of course, that's the scriptural way," he said.

Papa then asked Jakie what he and Johnny had been doing that day, and Jakie told of a disagreement with Johnny about trapping muskrats. Johnny insisted the place to put their trap was at the pile of dead branches and stalks the muskrats had built for their home; but Jakie thought the likeliest place was at the end of the boat, as it rested in the water.

"Well," smiled their father, "it will be interesting to see which of you boys is right. Personally, I think I would agree with Jakie!" He said he had trapped quite a few muskrats over at the creek when he was a boy.

In the mellow light of the kerosene lamp, Betsy enjoyed this fellowship with her family; but she couldn't help wondering why her father should have a fear that she might become unequally yoked with the world. Shortly she was to become aware of the dire concern of others also.

The following week, the presiding elder of the Shady Gap congregation chided Elder Brecher for permitting Betsy to participate in all the extra activities at school. A sharp thrust was made by one of the younger brethren who recently had been elected a preacher by the local congregation. He chided Elder Brecher that since an elder is one who "ruleth well his own house," what would the congregation think of him for letting his daughters "live like the world"? The confident young man was so bold as to cite Laura's missing church service often and Betsy's being "head over heels" in high school activities.

Instead of resisting this nagging, Elder Brecher, who was a kindly disposed man and wanted to keep the peace, was willing to see wherein he might be blameworthy. But then Presiding Elder Mitchell said to him that, because of pressure from some brethren and sisters, he was going to call a council meeting of the whole congregation to determine how active the young people of Old Order families should be in high school and among the people in town.

That evening at home Elder Brecher talked to his wife and daughters about the council meeting being planned, and about the criticism from the elders, even from some of the younger ones.

"Well, Betsy and Laura," he said, looking earnestly at the two downcast girls, "I want you both to grow naturally into being good and faithful members of the Old Order church, not because of restrictions made at a council meeting. But I sometimes wonder if you ought to have all those friends in town."

"The fact is, Papa, I'm not so popular as they make out," Betsy tried to explain. "It's much the doing of Elder Shrock's son, Nathan. He tried so hard to be at the head of everything, but the students wouldn't have him. Now he has been sulking and nagging at me for being popular with them. If the Old Order church would have a Sunday school for the young people, like the Dunker church in town, they would not have idle time to be envious. It's simply that I have some very nice friends."

Elder Brecher shook his head wearily. "But they must not keep you from becoming a sister in the Old Order."

Laura broke in vehemently, "Why do you allow yourself to be badgered by some bigoted elders and narrow-minded church members! Why don't you withdraw from the Old Order? We could join the Dunker church in town."

"No, Laura," he replied, controlling himself with effort. "I've always been an Old Order at heart and I always will be."

Within a few weeks the council meeting was held in the Harshberger meetinghouse, which was crowded with all the members for the two sessions each day. The meeting on the second and final day became almost stormy, as a few dissatisfied, complaining souls contended against Elder Brecher for being too lenient with his daughters. Their vehemence was more potent than his mildness, although he was defended by some of the more substantial members, especially by Elders Stover and Mack, and by his brother-in-law, Elder Abram Schaff, from Maryland, who emphasized the practice of moderation and manifesting a loving, forgiving spirit. Elder Brecher himself spoke briefly, saying he had hoped his daughters would join the church and had urged them to do so, but he would never compel them against their will. He cited Scripture to support his view. As for Betsy's extra activities at high school, he thought such activity and associations could not be harmful and might, on the contrary, be helpful to her. As for accusing him of being proud because of becoming rich, he said he had worked hard all his life and was simply fortunate in making investments. He explained that from early boyhood he had been skillful in earning money, yet he aimed never to become too fond of it but to cherish spiritual values above material. He hoped to be always a faithful minister to the local congregation.

This defense by Elder Jacob Brecher might have been effective with the members had it not been counteracted by a fiery speech by Elder Shrock, who spoke as soon as Elder Brecher sat down.

His powerful voice and fierce expression gripped the attention of all the members as he pleaded with them, "Save our beloved church from being swept by the current of worldliness into weakening compromises. In a crisis like this, one must not let personal relations interfere with one's judgment. I would not want to offend my dear brother, but when the welfare of the church is at stake, I must be loyal to the church. Our brother says he has been eager for his daughters to join the church, but why has he not done something to keep them from becoming more and more worldly-minded? How would a father serve the spiritual welfare of his daughter when he lets her go to a Philistine college to hear worldly music, and lets her associate with worldly people in town who exhibit paintings in their home that are far from being spiritual. I'm not divulging any secrets, mind you, for his daughter talked openly to her friends at school, saying how she listened to such music and was fascinated by such paintings. I appeal to you to save our church before it is too late."

Elder Shrock's appeal had a stunning effect on the members, who were swayed by it and voted to approve a resolution that the children of Old Order parents must not take an active part in extracurricular activities in high school.

During the two days of hectic meetings at the church, the households of Elders Brecher and Butterbaugh lost their customary quietude as the family gathered now in the one home, now in the other, to eat and to talk and to argue with each other over the proceedings. Four of Jacob Brecher's sisters and their husbands had driven up from their homes in Maryland, two of the husbands being elders in their respective congregations.

Now that the meetings were over, they gathered together for the final time in Jacob's home. Betsy busied herself in the kitchen to avoid further involvement in their discussions and to contemplate what might be the outcome of the council meeting's resolution. There was a constant hum of voices from the adjoining sitting room. Now and then a voice raised in argument with her Aunt Mattie, and Betsy could hear her name mentioned.

Finally, three of her aunts came out and sat on the long wood box next to the stove. Sympathetically they said they hoped Betsy wouldn't mind the complaining done at council meeting about her being a part of the world. They couldn't agree with Aunt Mattie, who contended that Betsy's father had been entirely too lenient with both the girls and that he should have compelled them to join the church by age fourteen.

Betsy could hear Aunt Mattie's shrill voice saying, "Jacob, the only sure way to get Betsy into the church would be to get her married to a young brother in the Old Order, like Paul Honstein in our congregation in Maryland."

When Jacob Brecher demurred, Sister Mattie offered substantial reasons why Betsy should accept Paul. "He's now twenty-one and has been farming successfully since he was fifteen, when he quit school. If Betsy would want a big man, why, Paul's the man for her, since he's every bit as tall as you, Jacob, and strong as an ox. His mother was a sister of my husband, Abram."

As Elder Brecher had often experienced, his sister Mattie was a formidable opponent in any dispute. She was a tall, thin, imperious-looking woman with a Roman nose and greenish eyes that flashed ominously, and she expressed herself with unmistakable force.

When Betsy heard this discussion going on in the front room, she went in and said, "But don't you see, Aunt Mattie, I'm not one bit interested in getting married. Papa has agreed I'm to teach in the public school, and I need to go to college in order to do that."

"Ach, Betsy," Aunt Mattie gave a little laugh, "you wouldn't need to bother about the marriage! Your pop could arrange all such things for you. But you ought to be ashamed," she said in an even more shrill voice, "to talk about going to college when the Old Order people have always been against such worldliness!"

"No, Mattie," Elder Brecher said firmly. "She has my promise to go to college for at least one year. She'll make a good teacher. But I'll tell you what I'll do, I'll drive down to your place and meet this young brother and see what I think of him."

Mattie was still fiery. "Well, you'd better come with your mind open to approve of Paul. I don't have any confidence in you, Jacob. It's no wonder you're in such a bad fix up here!"

Uncle Abe said that, of the elders present, he believed not one would disagree with Jacob that Betsy should go to college if he thought she should.

But Mattie was not to be silenced. She insisted that her

brother Jacob must certainly plan for Betsy's marriage to Paul after her graduation from high school the next spring. "This is necessary in order to restore Jacob's good name as an elder and to take care of Betsy's future. It would save her from having to go to college and be a teacher, for Paul knows how to earn money and save it still," Aunt Mattie attested.

In spite of the sick spells Betsy's mother had suffered the past month, she was forcible in declaring, "Betsy herself must have something to say about getting married. We'll have enough trouble with this dreadful decision against her taking part in things at school, and I do hope Jacob won't pay any attention to it."

"Why, Beckie Brecher!" shouted Mattie, eyes flashing and voice rasping, "You know well enough you can't ignore a decision like this! When a majority of the members speak, they must be listened to. If Jacob ignores it, he'll be in disgrace not only in this congregation but in all the neighboring ones. The only way to restore his good name, I tell you, is to have Betsy join the church and marry a brother—and the sooner the better!"

Elder John Butterbaugh, whose wife Salina was a sister of Betsy's mother, smiled as he suggested that all the troubles had been threshed over from every conceivable point of view. "Come," he said, "it's time to walk over to my house for the good supper Salina went straight home from meeting to get." He quickly succeeded in obtaining a calm compliance.

During the meal, whenever Mattie tried to start an argument, Uncle John put a stop to it in his benign way. "Now, Mattie, we've done all the arguing there was, and now it's time to eat the meal in peace."

But Mattie's husband, Uncle Abe, said he wanted to make an observation. "If people of the world had heard Brother Shrock's harangue, they would say our church was a failure, that the members weren't manifesting the love of Christ. I feel that Brother Shrock's remarks indicate how just one man can cherish ill-will against his neighbors. I would venture to say that for every one who is carnally-minded, there are five who are spiritually-minded. I hope and believe that the tirade does not reveal the spiritual state of our church, although his forcefulness did influence the voting."

"Yes, Brother Abe, it's good of you to say this; and I feel sure you are right in your observation," said Jacob Brecher.

After the family ate heartily of the Pennsylvania-Dutch supper of sausage, fried mush, apple fritters and apple pie, simple good heartedness prevailed. The folks from Maryland then left for their homes.

As Elder Brecher walked home with his wife and Betsy and the boys, his face had grown weary, his voice was hollow. Whenever mention had been made of Laura, they had been reminded of her outburst at breakfast that she couldn't stand to hear another word of argument and wouldn't come home until evening. Her father lamented that Laura had been coming home late rather often.

Because of her writing talents, Laura had been promoted to the position of society editor of the *Blue Ridge Zephyr*. Recently she had become fond of a young man on the staff, Sidney Longstreet, from Harrisburg. She did not tell her father of her friendship with Sidney, but he learned of it the day before the council meeting, when someone remarked to him in jest at Zeke's store that he could see Jacob was going to have a son-in-law! When he learned the facts behind the jest, Elder Brecher was too dismayed to know what to do. At home he declared that he would never have believed Laura would deal thus with him. She explained that she hadn't told her father because she didn't want to bother him with trivial conversation about how much she enjoyed talking to Sidney.

Elder Brecher was one who instinctively liked to have the approval of his fellows. Later that night, when he talked privately with his wife, he admitted that he was dismayed by the showing of so much opposition in the final vote. The perverseness of his sister Mattie upset him too. He remarked

solemnly that Laura's disobedience was possibly God's way
of getting him to heed the decision of the council meeting.
He believed that God was holding him accountable for being
too lenient with his daughters.

Beckie was shocked that he would take a stand against his
family in order to appease a set of misguided people. "Anyhow, Jacob, you ought to realize much of this comes from
jealousy. Nathan Shrock is jealous of Betsy, and you've found
out some are jealous of you since you've done so well in
money matters. And when people are jealous, they will find
something to complain about, like complaining about Betsy
at school. There isn't a better girl anywhere, and it's a sin
to be finding fault with her."

Elder Brecher remained unmoved, though he was well
aware of the jealousy of some members. "But that is not the
sole cause of the trouble. I've been thinking so much the
last few days about my own boyhood experiences when I
had sharp differences with my father, who was also an elder.
He reproved me for wanting to do worldly things, like when
I was so fond of Susanna Dietrich on the next farm. Father
didn't approve because her family were Methodists. I obeyed
my father, and after a while I understood that it was good
that he had been so strict. It's a sin for an elder not to be
faithful in ruling his own house. I'm going to take a firm
stand and tell Betsy and Laura that they're only to associate
with young people within the Old Order church."

"Ach, Jacob, how can you think it! It would be most unnatural to expect Betsy and Laura to give up the friends
they've made in town. As for your own father's decision
about the girl on the neighboring farm, I'm glad your pop
kept you from marrying that Dietrich girl, but you ought to
see that the two cases are entirely different." She reminded
him how both of them had found satisfaction in Betsy's success at school and the joy she had with pleasant friends. "If
you become too strict, you might turn the girls against being
religious at all."

But Elder Brecher observed he ought to be faithful to his calling as an elder. "We believe we are called to belong to our church, and you know how from the beginning a true Old Order is never to permit the world to inveigle him."

"Yes, but Jacob, why not be practical about this? Betsy will be better off if she has such refined girls as friends."

"Maybe so, but you should look to the deeper matter and ask her if her association with those refined girls will entice her away from our church. She actually said she's against putting on the plain garb because her friends in town wouldn't like it, or words to that effect."

"The thing to aim at, Jacob, is for Betsy and Laura to have reverence and love for God at the very heart of their life. Then if they want to be Old Order or go elsewhere, that will be for them to decide."

"Beckie! Beckie! Beckie!" exclaimed her husband, as he struck his knee with his hand. "Can it be you will so easily throw aside your loyalty to our beloved church?"

"Oh, not at all!" replied Beckie with considerable feeling. "I'm a devoted sister of the Old Order and feel at home there, but that doesn't say that Betsy and Laura would feel at home there."

"But that isn't the Old Order way to raise children!" he observed sternly. He was standing at the foot of the stairway. "I must remember and you ought to remember that it's the bounded duty of an Old Order so to raise his children that they all become Old Order and not something else!" His parting word before going upstairs revealed his determination. "I am going to be loyal to my pledge to the congregation when I was ordained as an elder and will heed the decision of the council meeting, painful as it may be."

4

Old Order Segregation

ON OCCASION, while Betsy was washing dishes, Jacob Brecher would sit down in the kitchen and talk to her. Whenever he had a concern about something, she could tell from a melancholy expression in his eyes when the serious moment had come. More than once he had been surprised and pleased at the wisdom she showed for her age, for she had an eager mind and kind, steady disposition. On the morning following the council meeting resolution, Jacob hoped that his daughter would show her usual wisdom and kindness in meeting the request he had to make of her.

As he sat in the rocking chair in the kitchen that morning, he began rather awkwardly to say he didn't want to seem unreasonable but wanted to appeal to her sense of what was suitable in an Old Order family. "We are supposed to be separate from the world, you know, but in your high school activities you are really one with the world. I'd be so happy if you could bring yourself to see it isn't appropriate to be doing so much and to be associated with so many people outside our church."

"Oh, Papa, I've had such a pleasant time at high school. Can that really be wrong?"

"It may not be wrong except that it tends to keep you from becoming a sister in the Old Order." His voice grew firmer as he spoke. "I want you to see I'm taking this stand for your own good."

Betsy was dismayed to see her father so in earnest. "I confess, Papa, I've given a great deal of thought about the Old Order church. But it won't help toward my loving it as my home if I have to give up my friends."

Her father caught his breath. "Betsy," he gasped out, emphatically striking the arm of his chair, "I'll have to take a stand for your own good, just as my pop did with me, and say once for all you must give up your friends outside the Old Order!"

Earlier, whenever Betsy discussed with her father the problem of the Old Order church, he remarked that, since she would be joining ultimately, why not think of the Old Order as her home church and love it as she loved her home? Now her father misconstrued what she had just said as sheer rebellion, that she would not love the church of her family.

She turned around to face him and was shocked to see an extremely severe frown on his face and his eyes so piercing, in place of the usual expression of kindliness she had always experienced. She felt like saying more but left the kitchen abruptly.

Elder Brecher feared he had not handled this delicate matter very well. He sat still, hunched over in his rocking chair, wondering what he should say when she came downstairs to go to school.

When Betsy finally came down, he noticed that her eyes were red and swollen. He said in a kindly voice, "Dear Betsy, you will see eventually that I am doing what is for your own good. That was exactly the way I felt about my pop when he denied me to go with the girl on the next farm who was not Old Order. But my, oh my, can't you see in the good mother you have that my pop was absolutely right?"

"But Papa, I can't see how it would help for me to give up my friends."

Betsy had to hurry down the lane to join the other girls as

they walked to town to the high school. As she talked with Martha from the next farm, she couldn't keep from mentioning her father's decision. "I'm afraid that he may hold me to it this time."

Martha thought she saw tears in Betsy's eyes. With a sympathizing tone she said, "My mother told me once that your grandfather was very strict. I guess your pop comes by it naturally."

"I doubt that, Martha, but this morning he didn't seem like the person I have always known him to be."

That morning in school, Betsy had difficulty concentrating on her studies. Her mind wandered often. She thought of the recent tea at Mrs. Grace's home, given in honor of the girls' chorus. She enjoyed being with her friends and meeting new people. Mrs. Grace and Mrs. Mellers had encouraged Betsy to be even more active in social affairs. But now she feared that her father would not relent, and she would have to give up all her friends who were not of the Old Order.

As Betsy walked home after school, she noticed nothing of the lovely countryside, though for the past few weeks she had been thrilled to watch in the fields of the Funk farm and the Strickler farm the myriads of little white asters just a few inches above the ground and the profusion of goldenrod rising above the asters. There had been no frost yet and her mother's dahlias were brilliant in the sunshine, but for the first time Betsy failed to notice them.

When she entered the house, her father asked her to sit down with him in the kitchen. He tried once again to explain why he had taken such a firm stand. First of all, he emphasized that he loved her just as dearly as he always had. Then he reminded her that in every Old Order family of good standing the young people are supposed to find their friends only among the members and their children, and he assured her that all of them would be happier after adjusting "to the practices and customs of the Old Order." He explained

in detail his boyhood experiences and his eventual joy and
peace in finally yielding to his own father's demands.

Betsy was relieved by his gracious manner this afternoon;
he was like her dear old papa once more. He eased her mind
when he asked, "Don't you have any pleasant recollections
of the Old Order? Doesn't any of it give you happiness?"

"Oh yes," she replied. "It is so pleasant on Sunday morn-
ings when you stand up to preach, and I enjoy hearing the
other elders. Family worship every morning is a blessing,
too. I like it when you read the Scripture to us and then
pray. Most of all I like singing a hymn or reciting a psalm
before we begin our work for the day."

"Well, tell me then, Betsy, what is in the Old Order practice that would keep you from feeling at home there?"

"Well, really, Papa, one thing that disturbs me so is the
ill-will shown by some members in always criticising others
for being worldly."

Being eager to win Betsy's confidence, Elder Brecher re-
frained from any arguing and said he wished she would pray
more definitely for guidance about her attitude toward the
Old Order.

While doing her chores, she felt inclined to think somewhat favorably about the Old Order. She reflected that she
could listen to a scholarly address at school and follow it
without her mind wandering. This, she believed, was due to
the experience of listening to the three or four sermons each
Sunday, most of which—when she listened thoughtfully—were
inspiring and practical. She thought also of hearing one of
the girls at school complaining so bitterly about the terrible
stepmother she had to endure after her divorced father re-
married. Surely the plain folk had something in their favor
in advocating and achieving a quiet Christian home life.
And when she thought of Laura's experiences as society editor of the *Zephyr,* she pictured to herself the woebegone
frustrations of social climbers in town, and rejoiced in the

sensible and serene attitudes toward life that her Old Order training had developed in her.

The problem was still not resolved, however. She couldn't help thinking of the hectic, feverish sessions of the council meeting and the stark burden imposed upon her by her father about giving up her friends in town. She recalled the delightful party at Ethel's home with such pleasant conversation and music.

She and Ethel sang, and Doris accompanied them on the piano. How could she ever give up her good friends? As for friendships with the boys, these had been few and always very casual. She was rather indifferent concerning them, for she was intent upon further education.

The problem of worldliness was a disturbing one! She would often ask herself why it was "worldly," and forbidden to listen to the piano or to have any musical instruments in the home or pictures on the walls? Wouldn't it be better for the elders to permit a person to participate for God's glory with the talents given by Him?

There were times when Betsy felt as if she were being tossed about between her loyalty to her father, whose prestige as an elder was jeopardized, and the natural inclinations of a vivacious girl who had come to love music, art, and literature. Her father did not again show the grim severity of their early morning encounter but continued to speak persuadingly to her. Betsy one day quoted some views from the tracts Mrs. Beinbrecht had given her, such as the freedom one gains by belonging to the Lord, but instantly her father was aroused. "If you have a church, you've got to have order, or else you run the risk of having anarchy!" he warned.

Disagreement with her father always pricked Betsy's conscience. It was instinctive in her to look up to him as the head of their home. But her father must have felt a pricking of conscience also, for he made a concession. He would agree to her continuing in the chorus if she gave up her position as secretary of the senior class. As she was so fond of singing, she knew she would much prefer belonging to the chorus than holding an office. It was difficult to explain to her classmates why she had to resign. She revealed to her closest friends her father's desire for her to give up all her friends at school. Much to her surprise, the girls respected her for wanting to be loyal to her family and church, though they insisted some other solution might possibly be found to satisfy her father. Had they teased and laughed at her, separation would have been made easier. In showing their love for her, it almost broke her heart.

One day at school, Samantha Reddig ran into Betsy. "Didn't I tell you you were worldly!" she taunted. "Now the whole church has voted that you are worldly and must change your ways."

Betsy looked at her firmly. "Well, Samantha, if it gives you any satisfaction to be cruel, have it your own way."

Laura reacted to the tense situation with obvious rebellion. She avoided her father as much as possible and even refused to answer when he spoke to her. The demand for separation imperiled both her romance and career. Her position with the newspaper was a prestigious one for women of that day. Her bitterness toward the Old Order church overflowed whenever the subject arose.

One day Laura complained to her mother, "Betsy is so upset that she often cries herself to sleep at night. It makes me so angry at Papa that I feel like running away and never coming back."

"Dear Laura, please don't be so angry," her mother said, tenderly. "We all experience trials and tribulation in life. We must have love in our hearts and faith in God to face hard times."

Betsy and Laura often talked at night after going to bed and turning off the kerosine lamp. Laura berated her father for his stand that she must give up Sidney. She said she couldn't do it because she loved Sidney, and he seemed to love her. When Betsy asked Laura if it might not be wise to obey their father, Laura exclaimed, "You have never been in love and simply don't know what it would mean for me to give up Sidney!"

"No, I have never been in love. But I have met some young men who have seemed very pleasant and interesting—Dave O'Lear, for example. I admire him greatly."

"Well, isn't that odd, Betsy!" replied Laura. "For, you know, I've thought several times how nicely you and Dave would suit each other. Where did you see him, Betsy? You've never mentioned him to me."

"Well, of course, I used to see Dave up at Uncle John's when we were small children; but since he's older, he grew up ahead of me. Just recently, at that party at Doris's home, she placed Dave beside me at the dinner table, and I enjoyed his conversation so much! Then later in the evening, when Doris asked me to sing, she asked Dave to play the piano for me! He did it so well, and he complimented me so nicely."

"Well, you know, Betsy, his father manages the print shop in town and is one of the most important members of the Dunker church there. I've been told it is people like Dave's father who have done so much to make the local congregation much more liberal about matters of dress. His mother even wears a hat instead of a bonnet and has her membership in the Dunker church at Huntingdon where they permit the sisters to dress more modernly. They say Mr. O'Lear's home is one of the most cultured in town."

A week later, Laura was bubbling over with excitement as she confided in Betsy that Sidney had proposed and she had accepted. Betsy was happy for her but anxiously suggested that Laura tell their parents. At first Laura stubbornly refused, contending that they would never approve. A few weeks later, though, she managed to gather her courage and told them of her engagement. Their reaction was as she had feared.

Elder Brecher's face paled at the stunning news. With

great effort he sought to control his voice. "What kind of a young man is this that he cannot come properly to me to ask permission? This is no way to handle such an important matter, Laura, to ignore your parents' wishes."

"But, Papa, he was certain that you would not listen to him and would never accept him."

"How could I? Why, they told me at Zeke's that he's an Episcopalian, and they say that is the same as a Roman Catholic! And how could you choose such a man? Does the fine Old Order training your parents gave you mean nothing to you?"

"Please, Papa, I am thankful for all that you and Mamma have done for me. I do love you and want your approval."

Mrs. Brecher put her arms about her trembling daughter. "Jacob, at least we can invite the young man to dinner some evening," she ventured to suggest. "Then we can see for ourselves what he is like."

Elder Brecher refused sternly. "Laura often has refused our advice and now has got herself into this mess. She must get herself out of it by telling him that we cannot approve."

Laura pulled herself from her mother's arms and ran sobbing to her room.

That night Laura pleaded with Betsy to help her. Betsy agreed to meet Sidney after school the next day. She was impressed by his smooth personality and good looks. He obviously was troubled over the difficult situation at Laura's home.

Realizing how deeply in love Laura was, Betsy tried to reason with her father about his objections to Sidney. She explained how attractive and educated he was.

"He may be all that, Betsy, but those are not the important things to look for when choosing a husband. Is it not better to accept someone who shares your beliefs and will provide for you a happy, peaceful Old Order home?" Elder Brecher looked at her directly as he spoke. Then his eyes shifted and saddened. "If Laura should marry that young man, he would take her away from us completely. I admit I rebelled against my pop even longer than Laura has defied me in this matter, but when I finally came around to listening to him, I realized he was right and I was wrong. That's the way I feel about you and Laura."

Betsy was surprised that her father still cherished the illusion that Laura would join the Old Order.

In November, the local newspaper carried the story of the cantata given by the high school chorus. There was grumbling from some of the members of the Shady Gap congregation, when they read the praise of Betsy Brecher's soprano solo. The complaints only served to make Elder Brecher even more harsh and unfeeling in denouncing Laura's engagement to Sidney.

The worsening illness of Mrs. Brecher brought further anxiety into the home. The doctor, who was in his late sixties, was inveterately old-fashioned and critical of modern practices. He was satisfied to use his own dated therapy, which provided only temporary relief. Mrs. Brecher said she was glad he did not urge her to go to the hospital at Hagerstown, for she felt one went to a hospital only as a last resort. Betsy did as much work in the house as she could in order to lighten the cares of her mother. Elder Brecher prayed earnestly at family worship for her recovery.

Betsy's mind was filled with worries about her mother, and her time was filled with household chores, but she still had quiet times to ponder over the controversy between her father and the Shady Gap congregation. She was deeply impressed by her father's continuing acts of kindness to Elder Shrock, his most severe critic.

"Papa, how can you be so kind to a man who has been so mean to you?" she asked him one evening as he sat in the kitchen.

"When you belong to the church, you have the love of Christ in your heart for your brother and want to be of help whenever he needs help."

Betsy had to admit that her father's personal testimony was stronger than any objections to the Old Order church that she had yet thought of.

5

Ups and Downs

DURING DECEMBER the girls' chorus rehearsed for a Christmas program to be given at the Free Masonic Hall. Nick Mellers was the Free Mason in charge of the program. One day he spoke to Betsy to compliment her on her solo part; at the next rehearsal he stopped again to speak to her and asked where she lived. When she told him, he exclaimed, "So you're the daughter of Jacob Brecher!" He added that he had had business dealings with him, and they had talked in his office about many things. "He's a very friendly man," said Nick. "May I walk with you a few squares?"

"Well, my father doesn't like me to have friends here in town who aren't Old Order."

"Oh, we've talked in my office and had a pleasant time." Nick laughed self-assuredly. "He wouldn't object to my walking with you and chatting, I can heartily assure you!"

Nick was not the sort to be ignored by a young girl. Although he had finished college and become established in business in his home town, he had all the gaiety and charm of youth. He was good looking and had an ingratiating smile which showed strong white teeth and caused his dark eyes to sparkle. His talk revealed a quick wit, and he could more than hold his own in sprightly conversation. Betsy had heard the girls at school say that Nick belonged to a well-to-do

family prominent in social and business circles, and had lots
of money. They often spoke of him as "such a wonderful
man!" Betsy wondered why a person so successful in business
and so prominent socially should pay attention to high school
girls, but she supposed it was simply because he was in
charge of the program.

As Nick walked with Betsy, he suggested that she ought to
develop her lovely voice with professional training.

"Oh, but Papa would never agree to that! You know the
plain folk do not permit any musical instruments in the home
nor any fancy singing."

"Oh, but you shouldn't waste your talent in such a strict
environment! You'll have to be on guard to keep from being
nabbed by some of them," he laughed.

But Betsy said she hoped she would never have to contend
against her parents. "I think my father is resigned to waiting a few years before I decide to join the Old Order, but I
don't want to displease him."

One morning in the middle of December, Betsy's father
came and sat in his rocking chair in the kitchen, while Betsy
was doing the dishes. She knew he must have something
serious to discuss. Solemnly he asked, "Have you been seeing
and talking to any of the boys in town?"

She turned around and smiled. "I've talked a number of
times with Nicholas Mellers who stopped to talk to me at the
close of our chorus rehearsals. I told him you didn't want me
to have friends with people outside the Old Order, and he
laughed and said you would certainly approve of him all
right because you and he had friendly chats in his office."

"Indeed!" gasped Jacob Brecher. After a considerable
pause, he added, "Well, that was pretty bold! But he did
speak to me and said what an attractive girl you were. At any
rate, I guess I'd rather you'd talk to Nick than to Dave
O'Lear."

"Ach, Papa, you needn't worry. Dave is so occupied with
his music, he hardly knows that girls exist; though they say

he often dates Nick's sister, Dorothy. I talked to him when he played the piano at Doris's home."

"When was that, Betsy?"

"Oh, at her party last autumn. He did play beautifully! He said he heard I sang nicely in the chorus and suggested I ought to practice faithfully. Oh yes, he also said he hoped I would learn to play the piano. Someone at school said all he's interested in is his music and learning how to be a writer. He wrote an excellent article about a contemporary novelist which they printed in the last quarterly review at school."

"That is very interesting. However, Betsy, I'd prefer you wouldn't be friendly with Dave. Anybody who would influence the young people of an Old Order family against joining the church simply makes himself an impossible outsider!"

"Papa, have you ever thought you might be mistaken about that?" Betsy asked.

"No, indeed, there's no mistaking about it. Your uncle John plainly told me so!"

Betsy felt that both her father and uncle were prejudiced against Dave. It seemed more likely to her that they would complain about Nick, who was not a member of any Dunker church, but was in a secret fraternal society.

One afternoon when Nick walked with Betsy after a rehearsal at high school, he commented with obvious amusement that he had found her father a sharper man to deal with than he had imagined. "He always seemed to me to have a real fondness for people and to be friendly, but I get the impression he's not keen about my seeing you."

Betsy smiled, but she wasn't particularly concerned one way or the other. She could see that Nick was a clever person and could be entertaining, but she was not favorably impressed by his character.

It was hard for Betsy to be with her girl friends at school but refrain from going to their homes. Nor might she ask any of them out to her home. One day her father noticed that her eyes were red from crying, and he asked what was troubling her.

"You don't understand how hard it is for me to give up my friends in town. You just don't understand how terrible it is!"

"Ach!" he explained, "it may be hard for you just now but after you have changed, you'll be glad you listened to me." Then he told her again of the great distress he felt when his father forbade him to do this or that when he was in his teens and he acknowledged he had been sharp in arguing with him, but later on he came to realize his father was right and he himself was wrong.

Betsy loved her home and was thankful for its usual peace and quiet. She found many things to occupy her mind and hands. During the summer she found delight in arranging flowers artistically in bouquets and enjoyed having a pretty centerpiece of flowers on the dinner table, for which her father and mother complimented her. Now in December she used graceful dried grasses and seedpods or a flowering potted plant as a centerpiece.

She found satisfaction at home also by reading books from the high school library. Her instructor in English encouraged her to read widely in various styles of literature. Her father did not disapprove, because he hoped that someday Betsy would become a teacher and accepted this as part of her education.

She read such books as Cooper's *The Deer-Slayer, The Pioneers,* and *The Spy;* Longfellow's *Evangeline* and *Hiawatha;* and one of Tennyson's *Idylls of the King,* 'Lancelot and Elaine,' which brought tears to her eyes as she mourned over Elaine. She was fond of Hawthorne's *Twice-Told Tales* and spoke of *The Marble Faun* as her favorite of all of Hawthorne's works. Encouraged by her teacher, she undertook the reading of the six-volume *Life of Johnson* by Boswell. One thing Dr. Johnson said made her think of the Old Order. He opposed the use of a special religious uniform, saying,

"A man who cannot get to heaven in a green coat will not find his way thither the sooner in a grey one."

In her class in English, Betsy found Trollope's *Dr. Thorne* vastly entertaining, and soon she was reading avidly all of the Barsetshire novels and liked each one. She decided she wanted to grow up to be as sensible and lively a young lady as the heroines Lucy Roberts and Mary Thorne. She was as lively and vivacious as those fictional characters, but she didn't bother to wonder if she were as pretty as they. Though Betsy was an attractive girl, she had heard all her life about vanity and the need to be unworldly, and so had assumed it was not important whether she was pretty or not. But no matter how unworldly she tried to be, the boys were good enough judges as they noted her fair face with animated blue eyes, her thin but red lips, her small straight nose, her delicately colored skin and her curly brown hair. Her figure was slim and graceful; and she was a picture of robust health.

During the Christmas recess, Betsy was entirely cut off from any contact with her friends in town because she had had to decline any invitations the girls gave her. But this Christmas Betsy prized the fellowship she could have with her mother. She enjoyed baking Christmas cookies and several large cakes as her mother looked on from her couch. They talked and planned and remembered pleasant things.

Several evenings she attended parties in Old Order homes where some of the boys and girls congregated; but after talking with them for a while, she felt bored and lonely, for none of them shared her interests in music, art, or literature. Then some of the boys became vociferous in arguing about who was the best cornhusker among them. Betsy thought the matter was of no interest at all. She realized the boys were adept at farming but not at talking about outside interests. She remembered the animated conversations she had had with Ethel and Doris and the other girls in town.

One evening as she sat at home, she recalled everything that had happened at the Christmas party at Doris's home a

year ago. How excited she was in getting dressed and then
hearing her mother say she looked so pretty. That didn't
seem worldly to her at all. One of the high school boys got
a team at the livery stable and drove out for her. She had enjoyed being part of such a crowd of boys and girls at Doris's
home. Everyone enjoyed a Christmas reading by Mrs. Karl,
then they played games until their sides hurt from laughing.
She had been one of several who were asked to sing, and
Doris accompanied her on the piano. Doris's charming parents had mingled with the young people. Betsy sat at a table
with two boys and another girl for the delicious dinner, and
what a lively conversation they had! Doris invited Betsy to
her party again this year, but of course, she had had to decline.

In the happiness of the Christmas season, Betsy hoped her
father might relent in his opposition to Sidney. She suggested
to Laura that it might help if she spent more time at home,
especially in the evenings. Because Sidney was visiting in his
home in Harrisburg over Christmas, Laura did remain at
home. The mail each day, though, brought a letter from
Sidney, and Elder Brecher's resentment grew. He com-
mended Laura for being home in the evenings more than before and made it quite clear that she was always to stay home
in the evening. Laura was indiscreet and hot-headed enough
to exclaim to her father that she wouldn't stand for his "con-
trariness." In a fit of temper, she declared she hated the Old
Order and would "never, never, become a member!"

Instead of answering in anger, as one might expect, Elder
Brecher rose to his feet. His face was flushed and he pulled
at his long beard. In a calm, dignified voice, he said, "I'll
tell you tomorrow what I decide to do."

The next morning he asked Laura to sit down in the kitch-
en. Solemnly, he stood before her and said he would give
her "one week to put an end once and for all to this rebellious
friendship with Sidney." That night Betsy heard Laura crying and longed to do something to help her sister, but she

knew that nothing she could say would comfort her. The next day when Laura came home, she had nothing to say but at once became busy in her room sorting out her clothes.

Betsy hurried to talk with Laura about her troubles and asked, "Laura, what do you plan to do?"

Laura mentioned nothing of her plans but said, "I told Sidney what Papa said."

Betsy expected to hear Sidney's reaction, but there was a long pause instead.

"Well, Laura, if there's anything I can do, please let me know."

"Thank you, Betsy, but I don't know how you could help."

So Betsy left the room feeling unhappy and useless.

The next day Laura and Sidney went to Harrisburg on the train and were married in his home. Then they sent word to the Brechers. Laura's father was stunned! He walked the floor most of the day and night, and said again and again he wouldn't have believed any child of his could be so rebellious! "Betsy," he asked, "What do you think of such a self-willed sister? Did you ever suspect Laura might do such a thing?"

Betsy was plainly disturbed and her face flushed. "Well, Papa, I knew she was upset, but I advised her to talk over the problem with you. Then when I realized how much she loved Sidney, I knew she would never give him up. I guess I have to say I wasn't too surprised to hear from Harrisburg that they had gotten married."

Her mother lying on the couch roused herself to remark that Betsy was being as helpful as she knew how to be.

Betsy was sure her father had never before been so upset.

Two days later the families of uncles and aunts assembled at the home of Elder Brecher and were joined also by Elder John Butterbaugh and his wife in a consultation on how to deal with such a violation of family loyalty.

Betsy overheard her father remark to Aunt Mattie that he had seriously considered making a codicil to his will in which

he would give an extra sum of money to Betsy if she joined
the Old Order and married a brother in the church, but he
had decided against it.

"Well, I should say not!" said Mattie emphatically. "I
don't approve of getting loyalty that way! When I was fourteen, Pop told me to join the church, and I joined without
any question. You ought to tell Betsy to join the church and
get married to Paul, and see that she does it!"

To Betsy, her father's plan seemed like a bribe, but Aunt
Mattie's advice was even more terrible!

Laura scandalized her father further by becoming an Episcopalian. Because she had not joined the Old Order church
and had not been baptized by immersion, her father considered her lost; and after consulting with the uncles and
aunts, Jacob Brecher decided that she was also lost to the
family.

When Betsy visited Laura in town, she told her of all the
heated discussions about the elopement that she had had to
listen to, but she was glad to add that Aunt Salina and their
mother defended her by saying Laura would always be part
of the family to them.

Outside the family, the blame for Laura's elopement fell
heavily upon her father for his failure as an elder to govern
his own home; and he was under pressure from certain members, including now the presiding elder of the Shady Gap
congregation. Betsy noticed that her father was deeply troubled. She pitied him as she saw him walking dejectedly up
and down the kitchen time and again; then he would sit down
and talk to her, for he seemed to depend upon her for comfort.

Elder Brecher's anguish increased when his wife's condition was diagnosed as cancer. He prayed fervently for her
recovery. When the family doctor finally sent her to the hospital in Hagerstown, the doctors there could give little encouragement. Betsy longed to be helpful to her mother, hoping to ease her anxiety about the family. She managed to

cook the meals, keep the house in order, and do the laundry in addition to her school work, so that her mother could feel satisfied that everything in the home was properly taken care of. The operation on Mrs. Brecher did not enable the surgeon to feel too confident of success. He told Elder Brecher there might be a month, or maybe six months, of a respite when his wife would feel at ease, yet he feared there might be a recurrence of the disease. Betsy and her father drove to the hospital every day to see her, and sometimes the boys accompanied them. Laura and Sidney also called on her.

Elder Brecher drove down to Aunt Mattie's to inform her of his wife's critical condition. While he was there, he met Paul Honstein and talked with him. Upon returning home he told Betsy about meeting Paul and of talking to Aunt Mattie about the possibility of their marriage.

"Betsy, what Aunt Mattie said about Paul when she was here is all true. He's a fine, strong, powerfully built young man, and good-looking, too. He seems to have a nice disposition. From the looks of his farm and the way he talked, I'd say he's thrifty and clever and a hard worker. He'll be inheriting a good sum of money someday, too. Yes, he's a fine young man."

"Oh, but Papa, I don't want to get married!"

"Now Betsy, your mother and I don't want you to get married until you want to, but we want you to have Paul in mind when you do want to. We want you to marry inside the church."

"I'll be glad to have Paul as a friend," she said, hoping to change the subject.

"And some day," he continued, "maybe when you are nineteen or twenty and would like to get married, you'll choose Paul. He told Aunt Mattie that he would wait for you."

Within a fortnight Betsy had a caller. In the late afternoon, when she was doing the weekly cleaning of the kitchen, she heard a knock at the kitchen door and was surprised to see

Paul. Though she had never seen him before, she knew from his pleased expression that he was Paul. His face was red from blushes, and his eyes fairly danced. When she asked him in, he said he had to do some errands in town and hoped to come for just a few minutes to become acquainted. Though Betsy asked him to take a chair in the sitting room, he said he would prefer sitting in the kitchen so she could continue with her work. She sat down and took up her knitting. She smiled to herself as she thought, *I guess he wants to see if I'm a good worker.* Paul stared at her as if he had never seen a girl before. He asked about her mother, and Betsy related what the doctor had said. Paul said he hoped her mother might recover, then stood up to go. When Betsy shook hands with him, she realized how very tall he was—taller, she guessed, than her father—and she thought his thick brown hair and smiling brown eyes were attractive. The Old Order black suit he wore was just like her father's Sunday suit. She saw him to the door.

After he left Betsy decided it could be all right to have him as a friend, but she would have to be careful not to give him the wrong impression. By the Old Order practice, a girl and boy are friends only when they are destined to be married.

In the meantime Betsy's father, troubled by a concern over her future, made a codicil to his will in which he specified that the children's guardian, who was Uncle John, should have the right to withhold any funds from Betsy if she should ever marry without his approval. The regular bequest to Laura was cancelled.

6

Sufficient Grace

EARLY IN APRIL, Jacob Brecher set to work at clearing the woodlot of some dead trees. After chopping down several large old oaks, he and a hired man loaded the logs onto a wagon. When they began to haul them up the little slope to the lane, the load shifted, and Jacob was pinned under two heavy logs. Betsy had just returned from school. Hearing the other man's screams, she ran down the lane to Uncle John's for help. Uncle John and the hired man managed to free him, then they took him to Hagerstown Hospital. The doctor said he had a broken arm and several broken ribs, and had been severely weakened by the bleeding of internal injuries.

Betsy remained by her father's side for several hours. When he finally regained consciousness, he was obsessed with the idea that his accident had been a "judicial dispensation from the Almighty" because he felt responsible for all the troubles in the family. Betsy recited some of her father's favorite comforting psalms and then some verses from the New Testament, but his mind was troubled that he might lose his salvation because of his shortcomings.

"But Papa," she said earnestly, "the Bible says we can't earn salvation. It's a free gift. Don't you remember the exact words, 'not of works, lest any man should boast'?"

"But Betsy dear," mused her father, "the Bible says we are to be 'rich in good works,' and just think how poor in works I've been!"

It seemed so dreadful to Betsy that her father, who had always been strong in faith, was now so wretched and downcast that he was afraid he was lost. Her mind went blank, but out of the blankness one thought did emerge that God was able to bless him regardless of his confused mind. She grasped that one thought and said, "You know, Papa, the Bible says, 'My grace is sufficient for thee.'"

He smiled and said she was always a blessing to him. She tried to comfort him, but his condition was plainly worsening. The morning before her father died, she sat beside his bed reading to him from the Bible and he gave her a smile. But in the afternoon he became restless and had a strange, rather startled look. Betsy stood there as if transfixed. After a few minutes he became quiet again, and she heard him whisper, "Thy grace is sufficient." He died before dawn the next morning.

It seemed that the world had come to an end for Betsy! All the virtues of her father became clear to her, and she realized what a splendid man he had been. She was bereft of hope and sick at heart, but having to do the household chores took her mind off her grief temporarily. But when those chores were finished, she was again distraught, like one adrift in a stormy sea. As the responsibility of planning the funeral was left in the hands of Uncle John and others of the elders, Betsy was free to give her attention to her brothers and to the work of the home.

On the morning of the funeral, she rose earlier than usual. She let the boys sleep while she got out their Sunday clothes and started breakfast. She was sick with longing for her mother, and the harsh realization that this very likely would be done soon all over again filled her with dread. Jakie came down early and wanted to help Betsy. He had taken his father's death so quietly that without knowing it Betsy had leaned heavily upon the young teenager. Now she realized that he was suffering inside just as she was.

Betsy tried to think of something to say to comfort him but was unable; she needed so much to be comforted herself. So they worked together silently. She thought it would be better for Jakie if he had something to do with his hands. The neighbors were doing all the chores at the barn, so Betsy asked him to get his brothers up and superintend their dressing.

Laura and Sidney came before they had finished breakfast, and the two sisters had only a few moments together before the relatives began to arrive. The neighbors who were to prepare the dinner came, so there was little chance for Betsy and Laura to talk.

Betsy dressed for the funeral and had everything ready when the elders and members came for the brief initial service at the home. When they reached the meetinghouse, Jakie and Amos sat on either side of Betsy, and Johnny was next, sitting beside Aunt Salina. Betsy could listen to the sermons only with difficulty, as she was worn out with grief and uncertainties. She tried to control her grief for the sake of her brothers who clung to her. As the sermons droned on, her mind wandered to scenes of her early childhood, when she had been so proud to be the companion of her father. Amos soon grew weary in the overheated meetinghouse and leaned against her arm. She shifted her position to make him more comfortable, and he dozed. His sturdy body grew heavier, but she wouldn't move for fear of disturbing him.

Three of the sermons were by elders who dealt with Jacob Brecher's life as a minister and his service to the brotherhood. The final sermon was by the young brother who had been elected to the ministry the previous year. His harsh voice brought Betsy's mind back to the meetinghouse as she listened in disbelief, for he was using her father as an example and warning of the dangers of forsaking the Old Order ways and precepts. Betsy's heart swelled with indignation; but

still her father and mother were Old Order, and she would
at least show respect for the brotherhood. In her confused
state, she couldn't decide what was the right attitude to have.

After the brief service at the grave, Dave O'Lear and his
mother came to where Betsy was standing with the boys.
Amos and Johnny were close together beside her; Jakie stood
solemnly behind them. The grim expression on Jakie's face
as he left the meetinghouse had not escaped Betsy's notice.
People came to speak to them, offering condolences and help.

As Mrs. O'Lear came to her, she put her hands on Betsy's
shoulders and kissed her. "Betsy, your father was a good and
gracious man. Remember him that way."

Dave O'Lear shook hands with Betsy. "I'm sorry, Betsy,
more sorry than I can say." He would have taken Amos's
hand, but the youngster buried his face in Betsy's coat. Then
Dave turned to the other boys and shook their hands, and
said, "Your father has left you a memory you can always be
proud of."

When Dave O'Lear and his mother were in their buggy,
safely beyond earshot, he angrily exclaimed, "Imagine that
conceited elder tormenting those children! It was mean and
cruel and completely unnecessary! I hope Betsy pays no attention to him. I know one who is finished with the Old
Order. It was written plainly on Jakie's face."

"Dave, you musn't be so prejudiced. Many of them are
wonderful people. Just think of Betsy's mother and Aunt
Salina. And Uncle John is a fine person, too, even though he
thinks you influenced his sons to leave the Old Order. He's a
reasonable man, and I'm sure someday he will come to realize
his mistake."

Dave retorted, "That's doubtful. Even after I explained to
him what I had said to the twins, he just wouldn't listen!"

"Yes," replied his mother, "some of the people of the Old
Order are strong-willed and obstinate; but if you can convince them they have been wrong, they will acknowledge it
with humility. Then there are some who are most gentle and

spiritually-minded. We are indebted to them for many fine things. This family has such possibilities that I wish they could be given a chance. Do you think Uncle John will permit Betsy to go to college, as her father planned?"

"Well, I should think he would be honor bound to carry out her father's wishes."

"Besides," added Mrs. O'Lear, "I know Salina feels very strongly that Betsy should go to college."

Immediately after the service at the meetinghouse and at the grave, many of the friends and all of the family returned to the Brecher farmhouse for a dinner that was served to more than sixty. Laura and Sidney remained for only a few minutes before returning to town as they wanted to drive over to the hospital. Betsy wanted to go with them but realized she must stay at home. That afternoon she talked with a great many friends of her parents and couldn't help being moved by the obvious sincerity of their sympathy. It was comforting to realize that her father was really appreciated by the large body of the members and especially by the more substantial ones. It rather startled her to see Elder Shrock standing in line to speak to her, but he eased her mind at once, "Betsy, your father was a good man. He was a better man in the sight of God than I am. He didn't hold resentment against me for talking the way I did at council meeting, which showed he manifested the love of Christ to all, and he will be missed by everyone." Betsy said she appreciated his kind words.

Aunt Mattie spoke to Betsy that Paul Honstein was here and she must pay some attention to him, but she was occupied with meeting the many callers. Paul sat on a seat in the arbor and was watching her. She looked over and smiled at him, as she noticed his ruddy youthful-looking face, and sparkling, eager, child-like eyes. She wondered whether he could be an interesting person to talk to. She compared his appearance with Dave's and he was no more handsome and, of course, he was wearing the Old Order garb with no necktie and an ill-fitting black coat. He certainly lacked the re-finement that she had found in her friends in town.

At the close of the afternoon Uncle John took Betsy over to Hagerstown to call on her mother. She had steeled herself to have self-control, but the sight of her mother, pale and haggard, quite overwhelmed her and burying her face in the pillow beside her mother, she burst into the sobs that she had been holding back so long. When she could speak, she said, "Oh, Mother, I didn't mean to cry."

Her mother replied, "Hush! You have the right! We must not lock it all up inside, nor grieve too much, for we have hope, you remember."

Her mother seemed relieved that she could talk with Betsy, and continued in her weakened voice, "It will be hard for you, Betsy dear, but we are not asked to bear anything we don't have strength for, as you remember your father so often read that scripture at worship. It will be difficult, but Papa and I have always been able to depend on you. I am sure you will do the best you can, and you know where to get strength and guidance. Be strong for the sake of the boys. Talk to them about their papa, and especially about their heavenly Father."

Her mother made an effort to reveal what was on her heart, "You must carry out your plans we have made together."

Betsy interrupted to say, "I've been thinking, but I don't know what I ought to do about joining the Old Order."

"Betsy, you must do nothing now while you are so torn by grief and uncertainty. You must not feel you are in any way to blame. It is not so! God does not work that way. You must pray, and when the time comes, you must make your decisions by what you believe is God's will. And the boys too, teach them to pray, and to love God first of all, then nothing can go so wrong."

There were tears in Uncle John's eyes as he sat on a chair by the window and heard Betsy tell her mother about the funeral service.

Betsy wanted to be a blessing to her mother and succeeded in being brave. She kissed her mother and assured her that she and the boys would pray for her often every day. But after she was in Uncle John's buggy she broke down again, and could no longer restrain her sobs.

That evening Betsy's heart was torn. As she sat with her brothers she tried to control her grief for their sake. They followed her about asking questions she could not answer, for she was asking them herself. Still she tried her best to give the boys hope and comfort. The very next day Betsy began to be troubled in her conscience; something kept accusing her that in dealing with her father she had been too independent. *And wasn't I downright disrespectful? Can I ever forget hearing him say I was rebellious? What a shame I didn't appreciate Papa more while he was alive!*

Betsy had always had a bright, joyous disposition which was sorely tested now that life had become harsh and dismal. She found that crying solved nothing so she continued to do what her mother would expect of her and made herself as useful as possible. She treasured the talk she had had with her mother, and kept thinking of it as she worked. She found a measure of relief for herself by working in the garden. She hoed long lines of onions and peas as if her very life depended upon it, and she never before had been so intent on digging out the weeds. Remembering the inspiration and comfort of the Scriptures, she maintained the morning devotional time they had always had and helped the boys memorize psalms. Betsy was thankful that her brother Jakie was helpful, and thought he was very manly. He said little but worked with such energy that she knew he, too, was working out his emotions and grief. The only way she knew to help was to let him feel her sympathy and love.

Betsy's graduation from high school came after the funeral when she was still in a state of shock. She didn't go to the social functions she had looked forward to for so long and the Commencement itself was sad, because her father and mother were not there.

Mrs. Brecher's suffering had increased to such intensity that when she died early in June Betsy could not help feeling some relief that her mother was now spared any further suffering. She remembered her mother as she was years ago, the one she could always depend upon, who was so sweet and helpful. How thankful she was that God had given her such a fine Christian mother.

At the funeral in the same meetinghouse there was in the sermons more attention given to the riches of the glory prepared for the saints of the Lord, and Betsy felt comforted.

Even though Betsy felt as though her spirit had been crushed, she had to bear up under the problems and do some planning and consulting with Uncle John as her guardian. She was comforted by letters of sympathy received from a number of her girl friends in town. Ethel commented that Betsy had been noble in handling her very difficult problem, and declared "we love you all the more for your faithfulness to your parents."

That night Betsy dreamed that her father and mother were at home with her sister and brothers and they were having family worship in the early morning. Papa read a familiar passage of Scripture from the gospel of John, "that they may behold my glory which Thou hast given me," and in his prayer he exalted the Lord as the Lord of Glory and thanked Him "for leading our children to love Thee and always to put their trust in Thee." He closed the prayer by asking "that our children might love the Old Order brotherhood." Then he said "Amen." In her dream, mother prepared such a good breakfast, as always, and they all had a pleasant time as they talked about their plans for the day. Betsy was thankful for her happy home. Then she awoke to find it had only been a dream. She wept bitterly. After a time she realized she must be thankful for the happy home that had been hers all those years. "Oh, if only I had not argued with Papa and Mamma about the Old Order and had joined the church when they wanted me to!" She lay awake the rest of the night and could think of nothing else that day except the worship service in her dream and her father's prayer about the Old Order. During the day Betsy realized that she couldn't continue to be so downhearted. She began what she knew her mother would expect her to do—the spring housecleaning which had been postponed during the month of May. This was the first time in her memory that the spring housecleaning, which was the most exacting of all the housecleanings, had not been done during May. Although the three boys were working out in the field, Jakie and Johnny helped their sister after work hours by taking up the carpets and beating them out on the lawn, Betsy did the rest of the cleaning—washing the windows and the woodwork and sweeping and dusting, and putting things away for the summer.

While cleaning the sitting room Betsy remembered so clearly the living room of Doris's lovely home and wondered how it would be to arrange their room something like Doris's. So she placed the ladderback rocking chair beside a table which she moved nearer the window, and brought two spindle-back, plank-bottom chairs from the kitchen to the sitting room, and placed one of them on the other side of the table. But there were no pictures on the wall. She had saved the bank calendar of last year showing the Assabeth flowing into the Concord River, so she pinned it on the wall. She had some books from the town library which she placed on the table. After she finished cleaning the room she sat down and wanted to see how she enjoyed her newly decorated room. Then came a knock at the kitchen door. To her surprise it was Paul. She told him of just having finished house-cleaning the sitting room and asked him to sit down in the rocking chair.

"So you're going to read some books," he observed as he looked at the books she had put on the table.

"Oh, yes," she replied, "I had such an inspiring English

teacher at high school who encouraged me to read widely in literature. "Do you read in your leisure time, Paul?"

"Ach!" he laughed, "you know, there just isn't any such thing as leisure time when you work two hundred acres of farm land."

"But have you ever read any books?"

"Yes, I've read some in the Bible, but that's about all. I never thought to read other books, but I guess it must be worthwhile. Do you think I ought to read books?"

"Yes," she replied, "it couldn't harm you and you might get interested in many things you never knew about before. I'd be glad to lend you my copy of Hawthorne's *The House of the Seven Gables* and you should find it interesting to learn what life was like in that New England home in Salem."

Paul examined the book and realized it was a novel. "I don't know if it's good to read such a book, Betsy. It's just a story made up by somebody worldly."

She laughed, "Why, Paul, you ought to be ashamed to show such ignorance! This kind of a book is the product of an artistic, creative mind, and gives a true and imaginative picture of what life was really like in New England over a hundred years ago."

"Of course, Betsy, you know more than me in book learning and I will trust you. If you will let me have this book I will read it."

After he left, Betsy sat looking at her new room but she didn't feel comfortable about it.

Ach, this isn't as nice as the way it was before! She put the chairs back to their usual places and took down the picture from the wall. *The plain folk simplicity satisfies me much better; I wonder if it isn't more artistic!* She was wretchedly tired and began to feel guilty of disloyalty to her family. The happy times she had with them in this room flashed upon her and she recalled the vivid dream of the week before of her father holding morning worship here and she felt some remorse for having ventured to change what her parents liked to have.

Betsy drove herself to finish the house cleaning. By the time she reached the cellar where washing all the shelves that held the canned goods took so much time and energy, she began to lose her impetus. She finished the cellar early one afternoon, then sat down exhausted. Her fatigue brought depression and dissatisfaction. But a knock on the door aroused her, and there stood Mrs. O'Lear, who had come to inquire how Betsy was getting along. They had a refreshing visit. Mrs. O'Lear told of the flower garden that Dave was cultivating for her. Then she offered to help Betsy in any way she could.

The next day Betsy worked in the garden transplanting cabbage plants and sowing seeds of beets and carrots and continued at her work even after it began to rain, since she was eager to finish. But her feet became wet and her back and neck were wet when she came indoors. The next day she felt feverish and had a sore throat. Though she tried to ignore it by working, she had to give up and lie on the couch. When her fever increased, her brothers made her go to bed and they called the doctor from town who said Betsy had an attack of old-fashioned grippe. At night she suffered from sleeplessness and delirium in which she blamed herself for not having done all for her parents she could have done, and for not being loyal to her family tradition, but wanting too much to belong to the world. The world of art and music and literature had appeared to her as so very attractive, but in her delirium she blamed herself for harshly turning her back on her family. During her convalescence she couldn't free herself from agitation of mind as she tried to reconcile an allegiance to the Old Order tradition and also to the world of culture. She suffered agony of mind especially during the night as she lay awake and tried to reason about her problem. She could get relief of mind only as she thought of the kind-

ness of her father and mother, and of her father's talks to
her and of his sermons. But then she recalled how she had
argued with her father about the Old Order. She couldn't
keep back the tears. In her grief she declared she would do
anything to be forgiven of such rebellion against such a good,
kind father. Then she remembered how he had advised her
always to be kind to people with whom she dealt; never to be
mean to anybody. This recollection which seemed to relieve
her mind was a light shining in a dark place! She sat up in
bed and prayed that the Lord would forgive her if she promised by His grace always to be kind to people and never
mean to anyone. The feeling of relief that came over her
seemed to indicate that the Lord had heard and answered her
prayer. She lay down again and fell asleep. When she awoke
in the morning she remembered how God had answered her
prayer and felt peace of mind for the first time in days.

7

The Move to Maryland

TOWARD THE END OF JUNE, Uncle John brought the news that the Brecher farm was to be rented to a family. He would take the three boys to his farm and Betsy was to spend some time at Aunt Mattie's.

"Oh no! Uncle John!" she exclaimed, "I'd rather work in a factory from morning till night than live with Aunt Mattie. I've never even been able to get along pleasantly with her on a short visit because we don't see eye to eye on anything. How can I bear to live with her?"

"Ach, Betsy, it won't be as bad as you imagine. She wants you to come down and stay with her. Be a good girl and try it for a while. If it doesn't work, you can come and live with your Aunt Salina and me."

"But Uncle John, what about college? Papa promised that I could go!"

"I'll see about getting you into college, Betsy, like your papa wanted."

The respect Betsy felt all her life for her Uncle John made her hesitate to question his judgment, and she trusted him to bring her to his home if life at Aunt Mattie's became unbearable. It was instinctive in Betsy to have confidence in him. He was a mild-tempered man of large build and personal dignity, whose blue eyes under thick, scraggly gray

eyebrows were capable of a twinkle of fun, though usually
their expression was one of solemnity. His face was full and
florid, with a long thick, reddish brown beard and clean-
shaven upper lip. He was a man of few words who had the
gift of simple expression, speaking gently and yet deliber-
ately.

The personality of her father had seemed so potent and
exerted such an influence on her mind that she no longer
felt critical of the Old Order. She kept thinking of her
father's preaching and of the many talks she had with him.
She asked herself again and again, wouldn't she be happier
if she were a sister in the church?

Uncle John took Betsy down to Aunt Mattie's in his team
on the last Friday in June. While driving down, Uncle John
talked gently to her about joining the church. "Dear Betsy,
I wish you might realize how anxious we all are for you to
join and I'm asking you to kindly think about it and pray
about it while at Aunt Mattie's."

"I admit, Uncle John, I've never felt so kindly disposed
towards the Old Order as I have since I lost Papa and Mamma, and I will continue to pray about it, I promise."

Below the steep hill at Ridgeville, a few miles south of
Waynesboro, and just below the Mason-Dixon line, stretched
out the farm of over three hundred acres belonging to Betsy's
large, portly Uncle Abram Schaff with the patriarchal beard
and his equally sturdy wife, Aunt Mattie. They both welcomed Betsy and her Uncle John. Betsy was given the light,
airy bedroom in the rear of the house above the kitchen,
with windows on either side. In a few moments she had un-
packed and put her clothes into the bureau drawers and hung
her few dresses in the closet. When she came downstairs
she clung to Uncle John as if she were afraid that he might
vanish! She dreaded to have him return home without her.
He stayed for supper and Betsy sat beside him at the table,
and looked up at him affectionately. When he was ready to
leave Aunt Mattie's in the early evening he stooped to kiss

Betsy good-bye. She threw her arms around his neck and almost cried, "Oh, Uncle John, how can I be so far away from you and Aunt Salina and the boys and you so far away from me?" He tried to comfort her and promised that he and Aunt Salina would drive down to see her. As he drove away, Betsy waved her handkerchief until the team was out of sight, then hurried into the house and up to her room in order to quiet herself. When she came downstairs again Uncle Abe and Aunt Mattie spoke to her comfortingly. It was hard to be away from Uncle John and Aunt Salina because they reminded her so much of her own parents. It was good for the boys to be staying with them.

Soon, a lady came to visit with Aunt Mattie, so Betsy and Uncle Abe had a good opportunity to talk. Uncle Abe began by speaking of what a good man Betsy's father had been. "He always exalted the Lord in his preaching and he lived to exalt Him in all he did."

"Yes, Uncle Abe," Betsy confided, "I have been extremely critical of the Old Order because of their many man-made laws and continual criticism among the members, but since Mamma and Papa died I realize many of the benefits of the Old Order and find it easier to ignore the shortcomings."

"I'm sorry it's been so difficult for you, but I'm sure that if you faithfully read the New Testament and pray for guidance you will see what you should do and peace will come."

"Well, what have you two found to talk about?" Aunt Mattie wanted to know after her visitor left.

When Betsy remarked that they talked about the Old Order Church, Aunt Mattie's face lighted up as she began at once to urge Betsy to think about joining. She smiled her sweetest smile in telling what she would gladly do for her in making dresses of the plain garb and prayer caps and a bonnet, and she wished she would ask Uncle Abe, an elder in the Leiter's Run Church, to baptize her.

Betsy felt troubled as she realized her aunt would not like any hesitancy, and yet in the presence of Aunt Mattie her objections to the Old Order seemed to be revived. "I still haven't decided, Aunt Mattie. I'm praying for guidance, but I have not yet had any conviction to join."

Aunt Mattie looked puzzled and wondered if to wait for such a conviction could be a trick of the devil. But her expression changed and she declared sweetly, "Well, after you've married Paul I'm sure you'll have a conviction to join."

Betsy tried to make Aunt Mattie understand her mixed emotions. "It's such an important decision. I feel great reverence for the Old Order because it produced such saintly people as Mamma and Papa, but I hesitate to join the church and be subject to the dictates of the presiding elder as he decides what is worldly and what isn't."

Aunt Mattie replied that Betsy's mistaken judgment was due to her being so young, "but you'll learn as you get older. You should never forget the Old Order is the church of your family."

Betsy said, "I want to consider this problem very carefully."

"Yes, Betsy," said Aunt Mattie, "that's a good girl!"

To her surprise Betsy found that Aunt Mattie was a pleasant companion, and she realized there was something of real dignity in her. She had formed an image of her aunt from all the times she had been in arguments with other members of the family. Now she felt sorry that she had complained to Uncle John because Aunt Mattie wasn't so bad after all.

The very next evening Paul called on Betsy. She could see that he had taken great pains to be properly groomed. He had even gotten a haircut. But she couldn't help noticing the hurried job the barber had done, for he used the clippers too far up the back of his head with the bizarre result that reminded her of a skinned rabbit, whereas on the top and front, his dark brown hair was thick and bushy. Paul seemed more at ease than on his earlier calls at her home and could express himself more readily. He didn't even stare at her. They began to talk about books.

He said he had read *The House of the Seven Gables* and he talked of the sorrow an evil man like Judge Pyncheon can cause. "But my oh, what a ray of sunshine was little Phoebe, and you know, she reminded me of you." Betsy thanked him for such a nice compliment. Paul thanked Betsy for providing this pleasure for him and surprised her by asking what other book she would recommend.

"Well, if you really like Hawthorne, I'd recommend the volume of *The Twice-Told Tales*," and she gave her copy to him.

Paul observed that there are people today just as bad as Judge Pyncheon who like to harm others. "I was talking to a brother in our church who knew what he was talking about, and he told of people in the Huntingdon church who are trying to injure the Dunker church by getting members not to notice worldliness. It's all right up there for a sister to wear a hat instead of a bonnet, and don't you know, the same thing is happening in the Dunker church in town. The son of one of their prominent members is doing all he can to criticize our Old Order traditions."

"Paul, I don't care to hear you talk that way, and I should be glad for you to leave me and go home." Betsy knew Paul was referring to Dave O'Lear.

"Oh but, Betsy, I didn't mean to offend you!"

"I just don't care to hear such talk! The next time you call, let us talk about Hawthorne's *Twice-Told Tales*," she said with a smile, as Paul left the house.

Aunt Mattie got out of bed after Paul left and was eager to learn how Betsy liked him. She was shocked that Betsy was not more enthusiastic. "Why, yes, Aunt Mattie, I shall enjoy having Paul as a friend, but he mustn't come here and criticize the Dunker church in town."

"What could he have said that was so terrible, Betsy?"

"He said they taught the members not to notice worldliness and criticized the women for wearing hats instead of bonnets."

Aunt Mattie's face became red and she shouted, "You are the one he should have criticized, as unfaithful to the brethren as you are! You'd better start thinking of Paul as a husband instead of fussing at him. He's a good, thrifty farmer who will make an excellent husband for you. You'd better join the church like he did." She picked up her shawl and stormed back upstairs.

As Betsy prepared for bed she realized it would not be easy in an Old Order home to have Paul just as a friend, but she was glad she refused to listen to his criticism of the more liberal Dunker church which Dave attended.

The next morning Betsy realized that Aunt Mattie's anger had not cooled overnight. "Young people aren't interested anymore in getting a husband. You're not being practical. Paul is so handy and thrifty and handsome and he's such an excellent farmer. All the sisters in the congregation admire him for his kind-heartedness. You're just a foolish girl. I won't stand for any more of your criticisms." And so on and on she went extolling Paul and lecturing Betsy.

Betsy agreed with Aunt Mattie's appraisal of Paul, but firmly asserted that she wouldn't listen to his criticisms of Dave or his church.

Her mention of Dave enraged Aunt Mattie. "You don't seem to realize Dave's the evil demon who is trying to spoil our family! But you ought to realize that Paul knows what he's talking about."

Betsy knew it would not be wise to mention Dave to Aunt Mattie again.

A week later Paul came for another visit. He was enthusiastic about Hawthorne's *Twice-Told Tales*, especially "Gentle Boy" and "A Rill from the Town Pump." In the course of the conversation, Paul happened to mention something that Uncle John said about Betsy. She looked surprised and asked where he had seen Uncle John. "Oh," he admitted sheepishly, "I had to see him about a certain matter and drove up to his home."

"Well, goodness!" exclaimed Betsy, who suspected what he was up to, and decided to be impolite enough to find out, "I think you might tell me what was the certain matter you had to see him about."

"To tell the truth," admitted Paul bravely, his face fiery red from blushes, "I wanted to ask him if he would back me up in trying to win you for my wife, and I asked for advice on how to go about winning you."

"Oh, Paul," lamented Betsy, "No, I am really not interested in getting married. You see, I must get my education first. But we can be friends."

All the color left Paul's face as he stumbled to his feet in consternation, "But Aunt Mattie—," he stammered.

"Aunt Mattie has really nothing to do with this!" she interrupted him.

The next day, Aunt Mattie was talking to Paul's mother who told her of Paul's bold declaration and Betsy's disinterest. Aunt Mattie lectured Betsy, "No young girl has a right to decide such things for herself; she must obey her elders. Just forget about going to college and start thinking about marrying Paul."

Betsy tried to explain, but that was impossible.

Aunt Mattie launched into the account of how all four of her daughters had listened to her and married within the Old Order at a young age. "You are entirely too independent and it just isn't right."

Aunt Mattie only made Betsy wish she had not been so mild with Paul. She should have just told him right away that she would never marry him.

Aunt Mattie was no longer gracious at home but became harsh in scolding Betsy every day even though she did her work with the same care as she had from the first. She was dismayed but she thought with some relief of the infare to be held at the Knepper farm on Friday and Saturday of next week as a means of escape, for she remembered her mother's mention of attending an infare when she was a girl.

Sister Knepper patterned the wedding reception for her son and his bride on the old-fashioned infare popular among the Pennsylvania Germans when she was a girl. "It will be an experiment," Sister Knepper admitted, "but I would much prefer to have something out-of-date like an infare to having a reception such as the world likes to have."

Betsy remembered that her mother thought an infare was a pleasant way of entertaining one's friends for something special. Now Betsy thought of the infare as an opportunity to get away from Aunt Mattie's scolding for at least two days.

On the Sunday afternoon before the infare, Nick Mellers came with his sister Dorothy to call on Betsy. Aunt Mattie was curious to see Nick because she had heard Uncle John describe him as "up and coming in the business world." He made a point of being very gracious to Aunt Mattie. Nick spent most of the time telling about his trip to New York, a Broadway play he'd seen, some successful business deals and a bowling match he'd won. Betsy didn't care to hear him boast of his successes, but on the whole she found him entertaining and could think of him as a lively companion. He was certainly gracious in his manner.

Dorothy complimented Betsy on living in such a pleasant home, and said if she lived here she would never tire of looking at the mountains. Betsy politely replied that that was the way she felt about the lovely countryside, too. They also talked about college life and Betsy's father, who Nick said had been so fine-looking that he could win a stranger's approval without ever saying a word.

When Aunt Mattie left the room, Betsy felt free to mention to Nick that although she appreciated the influence of her Old Order parents and missed them greatly, she still did not feel that she should join the Old Order and associate only with the plain folk.

"If I were you," he replied, "I would never consider it, for a person as attractive as you would never feel at home in the Old Order church."

After Nick and Dorothy drove away, Nick expressed himself enthusiastically to his sister about Betsy. "Just as I've told you, Dot, you can see for yourself that Betsy is a most unusual person. She's pretty, of course, but she's vivacious, too, and has remarkable poise."

"Yes, indeed, for a girl who has never been in touch with cultivated circles and has never travelled, she has the most remarkable poise of anyone I've ever met. And yet she is sprightly too."

"I wanted you to meet her, Dot, because I've just about decided that Betsy is the girl I want to marry."

Dorothy laughed, "You'd better be certain first that her family doesn't have any Old Order brother in mind for her to marry."

"Oh, I've thought of that. I think Betsy would prefer a worldly husband to an Old Order elder any day. I'm more worried about Dave O'Lear as a rival. He used to talk about her all the time; now he doesn't mention her. That's a sure sign that he's interested."

"Well, Nick, you'll have to play your cards skillfully."

"I'll not let that Dave O'Lear get the better of me, I assure you. He makes me tired, being so persnickety about music as if he knows it all. I don't see how Betsy can stand him!"

"Oh, Nick, you're dead wrong there! I've been out a half-dozen times with Dave, and I can't imagine a more fascinating man! He's not conceited, as you imply, but he knows what he's talking about. I don't know if Betsy cares for him at all, but I do know he's eagerly admired by the girls and they'd fall in love with him at the drop of a hat."

"Well, if he's ever in love with Betsy, he'll have to realize I'm around!"

Betsy kept thinking of Uncle John after Nick aroused her

interest afresh in college, and she was thrilled when Uncle John and Aunt Salina drove up the lane later that day.

When Uncle John and Betsy were alone, she asked him about college. He had talked with a banker in town who was a trustee of the Brethren's Normal College at Huntingdon, where her father had hoped to send her. He promised to talk to him about admitting Betsy to school but warned that she might be drawn further away from the Old Order than ever before.

As usual, there was little for Uncle John and Aunt Mattie to talk about without arguing, but today Uncle John agreed with her when she declared how important it was for Betsy to like Paul and to have him as her husband. Uncle John agreed that Paul would be a fine choice for Betsy and that would result in her joining the church.

Aunt Salina and Aunt Mattie talked about the infare Sister Knepper was giving the following Friday and Saturday at which Betsy was to help with serving the supper and the breakfast. They reminisced of one they had attended years ago. Betsy asked about her brothers and how well Jakie was working for Uncle John. She tried to keep from crying when they were ready to leave Mattie's, and she did succeed in smiling and threw kisses to them as they drove away, but then she felt very lonely.

8

The Infare

EARLIER on the Friday afternoon of the infare Betsy went over to the brick farm house of the Kneppers to help with the cleaning, and after she finished dusting the various rooms she felt the intense heat of this scorching July afternoon. She looked longingly at the inviting shade of the arbor in the yard. Nothing that could be at rest was stirring except the bees that kept humming continually in the arbor and now and then blundered into the summer kitchen. Neb, the black tomcat, was stretched out drowsily in the flower plot at the edge of the arbor. Despite the urgency of the preparations in the overheated kitchen, Sister Knepper was as composed as the cat. Like the mother in Israel "who riseth while it is yet night and looketh well to the ways of her household," she had everything in hand, and looked neat in her plain garb. Her daughter Sally looked up with a smile as she kept turning the pieces of chicken in the frying pan.

Sister Knepper appreciated Betsy's help. "You've been a good girl, Betsy, and I hope you'll have a nice time this evening."

"Oh, it will be my first infare and I'm looking forward to it so," she called back cheerily. Then she started walking the two miles back to Aunt Mattie's.

When she reached the bridge at the turn of the road she

crept close to the bank of the creek which flowed with the barest whisper through the green watercress. She stopped and picked a handful for Uncle Abe, who was always appreciative of special favors. As she walked in the grass beside the dusty road she waved to him as he was working in the cornfield at her left.

Betsy could think of nothing but the party. She daydreamed of what it would be like. Sally Knepper had sparked her imagination when she mentioned that Dave O'Lear was coming. She had heard about him when he had come to help settle a dispute between the school directors and a teacher. Her father was really impressed with Dave. Betsy could hardly wait to see him again.

Betsy's daydream was replaced by reality when Betsy looked up and saw Paul's team at the house. As soon as she stepped inside the door, she heard her aunt's harsh voice say, "We're going in ten minutes, so you won't have any time for primping." Aunt Mattie had put Betsy's blue gingham dress out on the bed. When she demurred, Aunt Mattie scolded, "There's no need to be all dressed up in your best when you're going to be working. You must remember you lost your parents and must act accordingly. For one thing, I don't want to see you singling out any boy besides Paul. He's been waiting for you a good half hour."

She helped her get ready in the quickest possible time, and in ten minutes they were on their way with Paul in his buggy.

Gloom frequently smothered Betsy's joy like dense pockets of fog enveloping one in the night. She sighed to herself, *If only I didn't have to wear this faded blue gingham! I guess my hair never looked so ugly, the way she put it up, after she said it would take too long to fool with it.*

At the supper Betsy was serving two tables of six each in the sitting room, just behind the parlor. There at one of her tables was Dave, her cousin Ann and his brother Sam with three friends from Waynesboro. Dave was the gay, lively one of the group, whose humorous stories had the others laughing constantly. Dave had completed his undergraduate studies at the University of Pennsylvania and was now enrolled in the law school. Betsy's cousin, Ann, was the solid type everybody respected, whom Betsy always depended upon as a loyal friend. She was a tall girl with dark eyebrows and a chin too long for beauty, but her quiet and gentle eyes were large and expressive. She was never quarrelsome but could be firm. It was she who arranged with Sister Knepper that her group should sit at the table Betsy was to serve. Dave's brother Sam, tall and brawny, who did the farming for the family, had been paying attention to Ann ever since the O'Lears had moved out to their country home.

When Betsy held the large pewter platter for Dave to help himself to the fried chicken his eyes lingered on her sparkling blue eyes as he took time to talk to her. He remarked that all the people up at Shady Gap missed her, and it would be pleasant when she returned. Her face was radiant as she returned to the kitchen, but Aunt Mattie was there and scolded, "What trouble a girl can be! Always eyes on the men and on that Dave O'Lear! Why would you be waiting on his table!"

Betsy tried to speak but Aunt Mattie's voice prevailed, "We all knew that dressed-up boy would turn your head! He's no good for you. You're not to speak to him, do you hear?"

In the midst of the hubbub Betsy's head went down, like the drooping of asters after the first frost.

Then she straightened up, "Mamma thought Dave was very nice."

Aunt Mattie sneered, "One of those high-toned fellows, but nothing to show for it! Now Paul—he's already amounting to something and has a good income!"

From her place at the table Ann watched Betsy as she ducked away from her nagging aunt and out to the kitchen. "Aunt Mattie treats Betsy like hired help yet," she complained, "and she's determined to make her listen!"

Dave interjected, "If I were she, I'd make a bee-line for her Uncle John's."

His brother Sam spoke up, "Betsy had kind, considerate parents and never had to endure such a scold as this Aunt Mattie. If I were you, Ann, I'd complain to your father about it."

Ann said she certainly would.

The staid Dunker home of the Kneppers was bright with the gay-colored dresses of the girls. The lawn too looked like a flower garden when the couples congregated to play games in the long July twilight. Fleecy pink clouds were scattered about the sky after a golden sunset, and the air was soft and sweet.

Betsy gathered on her tray the last of the dishes from the table under the trees, enjoying the laughter and banter as the groups formed for the games, then was startled by Dave stepping into her path and taking the tray.

"Come, Betsy, it's time to play," he said with gay authority.

"But I must help with the dishes."

"Why, the kitchen is full of women," Dave remonstrated with a droll look. "There no room for another, not even for one as little as you."

She was on the point of replying when her face burned like fire and she reached hastily for the tray. "Oh, I must go. I'm sorry."

He followed her glance, "Yes, I'm very sorry! I had hoped you could play!"

She had not managed to get away soon enough. Aunt Mattie was at the kitchen door! The scowl that spread over her face seemed so out of harmony with her prayer cap. Her fiery look troubled Betsy. Betsy mumbled to herself, "If only she wouldn't forever treat me like a little child!"

Soon Betsy was busy in the kitchen in the midst of a group of sisters. Aunt Mattie helped Sister Knepper carry the dishes that were washed and dried back to the sitting room to the handsome corner cupboard.

After a time Betsy heard the shouts of laughter from a group of young people outside the kitchen door playing blind man's buff, and she took a half-minute from her work to stand at the open door to watch. When Dave was in the center of the ring, with his eyes covered, he had everybody laughing. As Betsy went back to her work she smiled to herself, *He certainly can be lots of fun!*

But after a time she had a feverish experience. Just after the other women left the kitchen, and she was finishing at the sink, Dave stepped inside the door to say hello. At that moment Aunt Mattie returned from the sitting room and seeing Dave at the door imagined some scheme to get Betsy away. She turned sharply upon her, "Didn't I say you weren't to be singled out with anyone, and see how you listen to a body! Come on, we'll get Paul and go home!"

Betsy's heart beat violently as she and Dave tried to explain that there was no thought of any scheme, but Aunt Mattie would listen to nothing as she kept on talking, her voice becoming more and more strident.

"Didn't I tell you in so many words you weren't to be talking to any other boys this evening! Why was Dave in here?"

Betsy flushed with embarrassment as she thought everybody must be listening.

"Come on," ordered Aunt Mattie, "we're going now." She issued from the room brusquely, refusing to notice Dave's effort to explain.

It would never have occurred to Betsy to argue with her magisterial aunt, whose eyes flashed angrily giving her the appearance of an Amazon.

Betsy's heart quailed before the scolding voice which mounted as Aunt Mattie walked with her to Paul's buggy.

"You're a vain disobedient girl, not yet eighteen, and talking to that dressed-up Dave when I told you not to!"

Betsy was foolhardy enough to say, "I never before saw Dave look so fine. He had just come to the—"

Aunt Mattie interrupted sharply, "Don't you know, Betsy,

you mustn't notice him looking so fine! That's a sin! A body that spends all his money on clothes can't possibly turn out good!"

When Aunt Mattie saw Betsy safely seated in Paul's buggy, she hurried back to find Paul, and in a few moments the two of them came and Paul was full of talk.

"Why, Betsy," he beamed, "I was hoping to play in one of the games with you."

"Yes, but when she won't listen," Aunt Mattie broke in, "she has to be dealt with."

But Paul kept talking about the games. The short ride seemed to Betsy to take ever so long and when they reached Aunt Mattie's, she asked to be excused, saying she was going to bed. Before Aunt Mattie could say a word, she rushed up the stairs like a flash and into her room, leaving Paul standing in the hall with her imperious aunt!

After she was in bed she recalled Aunt Mattie's expression, "dressed-up Dave," which gave her a clear image of him at the party; he was not dressed-up, but appropriately dressed. "Why shouldn't he look fine, and why shouldn't I admire him for looking fine?"

She was awake early the next morning and heard Aunt Mattie open the door and say, "Put on your work dress, Betsy, you aren't going over to Knepper's this morning!"

She reminded her, "But you promised—the breakfast."

"Don't talk of running to a party when there's work to do here at home!"

When Aunt Mattie went out and closed the door, Betsy broke into a storm of tears, and her heart was torn with grief and indignation. She asked herself why she should remain any longer at Aunt Mattie's!

She was busy in the kitchen when the four young men who had occupied the spare room appeared in the parlor and talked with Aunt Mattie before returning to the Knepper farm for the infare breakfast. After she saw them off, she was back in the kitchen and told Betsy of the plans for the day. As the list grew she stared at her in disbelief, realizing the whole Saturday morning would not see the end of the work. It was like an interminable trail leading finally to a dead end.

After doing numerous tasks indoors, Betsy scrubbed the porches, for which she brought water in buckets up from the spring house. The last bucket suddenly became heavier as she saw the sun sparkling on a team from the infare. Her heart sank and her unpromising hope of finishing in time faded when a whole cavalcade of teams flashed by, raising clouds of dust. She went on with her work slowly, sick with disappointment.

Then one of the carriages stopped and there was Dave getting out! He called as he crossed the yard, "Hello, Betsy, here we are, six of us, to help you finish the scrubbing."

"The porch will be spick-and-span in a jiffy and ready for callers," she called back smiling. Then she thought to herself, *Mercy! what a sight I must be!*

"Sorry we weren't here earlier, it would have taken no time and you'd have been over for the breakfast! We missed you—," he was going on eagerly when a second-floor window was jerked up.

"David O'Lear," Aunt Mattie called, "Can't you see Betsy's too busy to be having any visitors?"

He gave Betsy a droll sidelong look, then said gravely, "Betsy seems to have finished quite a stint, Mrs. Schaff. Perhaps I could help if she has more to do."

Aunt Mattie glared at him and dropped the window with a thump.

"Your poor aunt doesn't get much joy out of life, does she?" Dave remarked roguishly. Then he said to Betsy as they walked towards the carriage, "You're certainly in a dismal plight here!"

Ann called from the carriage as Dave got in, "Why not come up to Shady Gap?"

Betsy watched Dave's team as it disappeared. For that

moment she overlooked having missed the infare breakfast.
Cousin Ann's parting words sank deeply into her mind, and
during the afternoon she debated whether it would not be
right for her to run away from Aunt Mattie's to Uncle John's.
"Why should I put up with this scolding all the time?"

After early supper she washed and dried the dishes more
quickly than ever before so she would be ready when Uncle
Abe drove up to Waynesboro.

But Aunt Mattie frowned. "No, you can't go this time!
Anyhow, Betsy, you still have some mending to do."

Betsy felt a choking in her throat, but she managed to say,
"Uncle Abe told me this afternoon I could go with him. I
should very much like to go."

Aunt Mattie turned upon her husband, "What do you mean
by telling her that, Abe, after I told you Dave O'Lear stopped
here this morning! As long as she lives in this house, she's
going to tend to her work first!"

"Well," he replied, pulling at his beard, trying to smile,
like one cornered in a cross-examination, "Betsy told me she
hoped to see Uncle John in town."

"Pshaw! Such a goose!" she said scornfully. "Can't you see
it's not Uncle John she's wanting to see! Go, Betsy, wash your
face and get to your sewing."

As she sat on the back porch, Betsy looked up from her
mending to watch Uncle Abe drive away. Some tears fell.
Tammy jumped up on her lap, but she pushed him off. Then,
relenting, she lifted him up and his forgiving purr comforted
her.

After a time Aunt Mattie called from the kitchen, "I'm
going for the setting eggs. Mind, you work good and finish
your stint."

While the dusk deepened, she saw a flicker of light in a
house up on the hill. The orchard, wood lot and Ridgeville
soon were lost in darkness and she felt she was quite alone.
It was the last of July. As she rocked quietly, her mind went
over the first days here. Aunt Mattie, too, had been shocked

by the death of her father, then of her mother, and did her best to ease those terrible days. True, she filled every minute with work and was so eager for her to join the church and get married to Paul. She went over those experiences again and again.

She thought of Aunt Mattie's good traits: she had a kind heart, and no one was ever more willing to help those in need; she would sit up all night with the sick; she did lots of sewing for others; she never turned a needy person from the door. But of course, she could be very stern, and she must always have her way!

Betsy thought back over her childhood again at home with her parents and brothers and sister. She thought how fortunate it was that her brothers were together at Uncle John's farm at Shady Gap. *If Uncle John would only take me in too,* she thought, *it would be just like the Promised Land! I'd work hard. I don't mind the work here. It's just always the scolding; nothing ever done to satisfy her! It was good of Ann to speak this morning about coming up to Shady Gap. Maybe if I prayed hard, Uncle John would take me in.* She felt the excitement of her plan.

Betsy moved in from the porch to the kitchen and continued with her sewing until she fell asleep. She was awakened by Aunt Mattie's return but didn't mind so much that she nagged about her not getting much mending done and wasting the light. She thought to herself that tomorrow night she would be at Uncle John's. As she went upstairs, her step was as light as her heart. The old fear of Aunt Mattie seemed childish and long ago.

9

The Promised Land

BETSY WAS AWAKE long before dawn on Sunday morning and went over her plans breathlessly, estimating how long it would take to walk the eight miles or more to Shady Gap. Her excitement made it seem much farther away, and the dawn seemed reluctant to break on the horizon. As the light increased, the outline of South Mountain reminded her of the verse from Psalm 121 her mother often quoted, "I will lift up mine eyes unto the hills, from whence cometh my help. My help cometh from the Lord, which made heaven and earth." She thought to herself, *I know what my mother would say!*

She dressed as soon as it was light, so she could start breakfast early, which she hoped would please Aunt Mattie; but everything seemed to go wrong. She dropped and broke a plate, spilled some of the egg batter on the stove, and forgot to make the coffee!

After breakfast and family worship, Aune Mattie agreed Betsy might stay home from the morning service at Leiter's Run Church because she complained of a thumping headache and dizziness.

My head certainly does thump—and my heart too, Betsy reasoned.

When Uncle Abe and Aunt Mattie drove away in their

buggy for church, she prepared everything she could for the family dinner, but lost precious minutes cleaning up the broken pieces of a crock she dropped in her haste, and the peas that scattered everywhere.

Ach, I must slow down! she scolded herself, as she wiped the perspiration from her face. She already was feeling alarm that Aunt Mattie might return before she started on her journey and that made her head thump even more!

Now I must run! Oh no! She stopped suddenly. *I mustn't forget to pray!* She knelt by the kitchen table and asked God please to forgive her running away from Aunt Mattie's and to be her strength and help.

She wrote a brief note to Uncle Abe and Aunt Mattie saying it would be better all around for her to be at Uncle John's and thanking them for providing a home for her.

Grandfather Grumvine was sitting on his porch with his crutches beside him as Betsy passed. He demanded to know why she wasn't at meeting. She called back quickly, as she increased her pace, that she was going somewhere. Then she hurried on feverishly.

When she approached the old Amsterdam school house where the River Brethren held meeting, she was afraid to pass lest some of the brethren or sisters sitting near the open windows might see her and somehow get word to Aunt Mattie. She lost valuable time by going up several fields, to avoid passing it, and finally she reached the Baltimore Pike which ran east from Waynesboro to the Blue Mountain. *Church will not be over for a while yet, but I'll have to hurry!* She smiled with relief when she reached the road leading north to Shady Gap.

Ach, how my face burns and my heart thumps! I can almost hear Aunt Mattie's sharp voice!

She kept pushing on, thinking she could rest when she got near to Uncle John's. Presently she mused with delight, *Ah, there's dear old Burns's Knob! Mother used to tell us to look over at it when she was having us learn the psalms by heart,*

"The mountains shall bring peace to the people. . . . He shall save the children of the needy." That might apply to me now! I'm glad Mother had us learn the psalms! Everything up here is so wonderful!

Then she happened to glance back and saw a team far behind, and her heart pounded. She thought wildly to run somewhere and hide, but she looked again and saw it wasn't Uncle Abe's carriage. The fear that the next one might be his drove her forward. *When Aunt Mattie's provoked, nothing keeps her back!*

As Betsy kept looking back, she was unaware of a carriage drawn by two horses coming towards her. She was startled when she heard it stop. Paul Honstein greeted her joyously as he jumped out of the front seat. But there was fear in his voice as he questioned, "You aren't going up to your Uncle John's by any chance? Ach, Betsy," he pleaded, "I could make a happy home for you."

"But Paul," Betsy smiled in the midst of her consternation, "we can always be friends."

Paul's father remained undisturbed in the back seat beside his wife, who, however, got out and trained a severe eye on Betsy. "How is it you haven't been to church? We just came from Harshberger meeting where Pop helped with the preaching, and we're going to Brother and Sister Ressler's for dinner. Why are you away out here already?"

Betsy covered up her astonishment as best she could. "Oh, I'm on my way up to Uncle John's. I must see him about something."

"You mean you've run off while Sister Mattie's been to church?"

Sister Honstein was a thin, wiry woman with sharp black eyes and a determined-looking chin. Whenever she became agitated, she talked with her eyes closed except for a mere slit of blackness staring through. "Seems to me you'd better get in with us, Betsy. Your Aunt Mattie will be upset to find you gone when she comes home."

But Betsy said she must hurry on, and she hurried as she had never done before, running until she was out of breath, then walking hurriedly. She became almost panicky, imagining Sister Honstein rushing to tell Aunt Mattie. She felt she musn't lose a minute, yet as she approached Shady Gap she began to feel less tense and became more aware of the countryside and noticed how large the apples had grown on the trees of the apple orchards and noticed also the sturdy growth of the corn.

After what seemed to Betsy an interminably long time she reached the bridge near Shady Gap and saw Uncle John's farmhouse in the distance. As she hurried past the turn in the road, she glanced beyond to her own former home. But now her one desire was to reach Uncle John's, and there she darted to a break in the bramble-grown fence, as if to a place of refuge, her breath short with hurry and anxiety, her face sweaty, her hair mussed. She looked with desperate longing at the farmhouse that seemed so near across the cool green clover field, then put down her bundle. "Ach!" she cried, thwarted and dismayed, "fellows playing ball in there!"

Knowing Uncle John's very strict, old-fashioned views about the relationship between boys and girls, she felt the question flash upon her mind, *What if he saw me climb the fence and cross the field where the boys are playing?* At the same moment she heard a dashing team and was overwhelmed by the fear that Aunt Mattie might be right upon her! She grasped the top rail of the fence and gave a mournful cry, "Like even the Promised Land!—and yet—"

Disappointed, she grabbed her bundle and turned back to the road in order to hurry to the lane at the far end of the field when she was startled to hear her name called gaily, and looking back she saw Dave O'Lear run from the clover field towards the fence and lightly clear it.

"Betsy Brecher!" he exclaimed again as his lively brown eyes met hers. "You haven't walked all the way up from

Ridgeville in this scorching sun?" And then he added heartily, "Welcome back!"

"Yes. I've come to ask Uncle John to keep me."

"Ah, Betsy, when you moved down to Maryland, everybody said you didn't belong there. You belong here."

"That's the way I feel too!" She smiled back. The dimples in her cheeks disappeared and her face clouded, as she added, "You saw for yourself how things are at Aunt Mattie's. I'm hoping Uncle John will take me in!"

"I hope so, too!" he said, "But it won't help any if he sees you talking to me! You see, Betsy, I'm an outsider to people like your Uncle John!"

"Maybe you can get Uncle John to think better of you." Then she felt a great urgency as another team passed by, "Oh, I must hurry to the lane! Aunt Mattie's team might be the very next one!"

"Well, don't worry, I'll have these rails down in a jiffy! And now, Betsy," he said with mock gallantry, "just step across into the clover field and you'll be safe!"

"Thanks, Dave," she smiled as she stepped over the rails into the clover field. Her heart lightened; she was home! She turned back to him, her face revealing relief and joy, "Dave, it's so good to be home with Aunt Salina." She winked back the tears.

He said, "This is your place! Your leaving was a mistake. I hope everything will work out now."

As Betsy hurried across the field she heard the boys call, "Come on, Dave, and play ball! You'll never get the rails up if you keep watching her!"

After she jumped from one stone to another in crossing the brook that ran through the field, she saw Amos leave his play and scurry indoors. Shortly, Aunt Salina appeared on the porch, looking pleased. She was Betsy's favorite aunt, as she had been the favorite sister of her mother. She was kindhearted and full of understanding of young people, and had a winning smile. She was a medium-sized woman with lovely brown hair touched with gray, parted in the middle, over a broad white forehead. Betsy thought the plain garb was especially suited to a beautiful soul like Aunt Salina. In a moment she was followed onto the porch by Uncle John who looked a little questioningly down at Betsy as she stood on the bottom step. Ann and all three of the brothers hurried out eagerly to welcome her.

Betsy had meant to give an explanation of her coming, but her voice failed her as she stood below them. The tears overflowed as she said pleadingly, "Please let me live with you!"

Her heart moved into her throat and choked her as she waited. Uncle John's slow deep-chested voice had solemnity, "We have room yet for one of God's little ones." Aunt Salina gently echoed, "Always room for God's little ones already." The boys clapped their hands and called "hooray" as they rushed down the steps to kiss and hug their sister.

After Dave replaced the rails, he called to the boys that he was going over to his house. He walked across Uncle John's fields to his own home and shortly was seated at the piano where he played some songs by Schubert. When his mother came into the room, he told her of meeting Betsy at the fence.

"Well, good for Betsy! There's no keeping her down!" She asked Dave how Betsy was dressed. He said actually he hadn't observed her dress. "All I saw were those blue eyes that sparkled like diamonds in the sun. I declare it wouldn't be hard for me to fall in love with her!"

"But you want to remember that Old Order families attend to marriage today just as it was done a hundred years ago. Aunt Salina told me Uncle John has his heart set on Betsy's marrying Paul Honstein in order to make sure that she will join the Old Order."

"Yes, that is a difficulty, but since Betsy is the sort of girl I like best, sweet and intelligent and happy but never prim, I'll do my best to win her."

At Uncle John's, Betsy rejoiced that here she would experience good will instead of constant criticism. The bicker-

ing and nagging at Aunt Mattie's had been a bad dream from
which she awoke in a realm where loving-kindness prevailed.

Down in the kitchen on the ground floor Aunt Salina and
Ann put aside washing the dinner dishes to prepare a special
dinner for Betsy. And up in the sitting room she felt completely happy as Uncle John, sitting in his rocking chair and
slowly waving a homemade fan showed his approval of her
coming. The sitting-room was to the left of the wide central
hall and was a large square room with four windows looking
out on Uncle John's corn fields and the clover field and Aunt
Salina's flower garden.

There was genuine satisfaction for Betsy just to sit and
look at Uncle John, but it was even greater satisfaction to
hear him welcome her. She couldn't thank him enough for
taking her in. When she told how unhappy she had become
at Aunt Mattie's, he admitted he often felt he ought to bring
her back. Then she described how she managed to get away,
but said she was afraid Aunt Mattie would never forgive her.
Uncle John tried to ease her fears, however, by saying he
would drive down to see her Aunt Mattie and make everything right. But Betsy feared that Aunt Mattie would not
be readily disposed to forgive, and as she was to experience,
for more than four years her aunt cherished a grudge against
Uncle John for receiving Betsy into his home.

Betsy was shocked now to see her uncle's cheerful welcoming look disappear as his face assumed a troubled look.
"Betsy, I'm sorry to have to mention this, but when the boys
ran in to tell us you were coming, they said Dave was with
you at the fence. I was very grieved to hear that! No one
could be more welcome in our home than you, but I must
caution you again about him. You see, Betsy, he just doesn't
belong to our people and you know what a bad influence
he's been to keep our young folks from joining the church!"

Betsy felt her face becoming hot as she thought she ought
to defend Dave but decided that all she would do now was

explain about his being at the fence and taking down the rails so she wouldn't have to walk down to the lane.

"That may be a satisfactory explanation this once, but you know how we want you to marry inside the church, so don't pay any attention to him."

Before Betsy could reply, Aunt Salina called her to come down to the kitchen because her dinner was ready, and Uncle John went along saying he wanted to hear her tell Mom how she managed to run away from Aunt Mattie's. He thought that showed she had "lots of get-up."

After enjoying her dinner, Betsy eagerly inquired of Uncle John what the trustee in town had said about her going to college. Uncle John explained that although it was late for entering a student, the trustee in town was sure the college would be glad to enter Betsy because of her high scholastic record. She thanked him and said how pleased she was. He then explained to Betsy that although he himself didn't approve of girls going to college, he was doing this because her father had promised to send her. However, since he was going against his own judgment and his conscience was not quite satisfied, he decided to make her a proposition. He would send her to college provided she would promise him never to get married without his approval. "Of course," he explained, "your pop specified in his will that as your guardian I was to have a say already about who you might marry, but I would much rather you gave me your own promise." Then he remarked he had been alarmed by talk he heard at Zeke's store about the way young girls at college became engaged, and he asked her to promise she would not become engaged to any man before she became twenty-one.

Betsy couldn't see any reason why she should not agree to his proposition since she was not at all interested in getting married. She had her mind set on getting an education. She readily promised to do as he asked.

Within a few days of her coming Betsy felt at home, flew

about her work singing, kept the rooms tidied up, supervised the boys at their chores with fun and teasing, made a game of their work of keeping the wood box full, and helped them with their Bible verses. She became a playfellow to them and they were constantly calling for her even when she was busy indoors. They wanted to show her everything they did and especially their games. Amos wanted her to come out into the yard to watch his kitten beg for food like a dog. She showed she was properly impressed and made it seem very important to him. It was so good to be close to her brothers again.

Though Betsy was cheerful and busy with her work every day, when she was alone she was harassed by a questioning going on inside of her. She was surprised that it cost her something to run away from Aunt Mattie's as she found she couldn't get rid of a sense of guilt. *Have I been unfair to Aunt Mattie? She does have some excellent traits and since she's my father's sister, she should be just as likeable, but for some reason she isn't. What could I do to help her be more kind?* Though Betsy argued with herself that here at Uncle John's was the best place for her, she couldn't get rid of that questioning.

10

The Same Problems

UNCLE JOHN waited a few days before he talked to Betsy about the all-important topic of her joining the church. The following Sunday as he rested on the porch after a bountiful dinner he waited until she had finished helping with the dishes. When she came up to the sitting room, he called to her to come out on the porch. She guessed immediately what that meant, and recalled his earnest exhortation to join the church when he had taken her to Aunt Mattie's in June. Betsy was thankful that Uncle John was gentle instead of being harsh, but it dismayed her to see how persistent he could be in his gentle way.

"Betsy, you would look so nice in the garb of a sister of the Old Order. Why, you'd look every bit as pretty as your Aunt Salina," he began.

"But, Uncle John, I feel much better about dressing modestly in the current fashion and not being so different from other people."

"Yes, but after you've been baptized and joined the church, your heart will be changed and you won't mind being different. You will be pleased that you are a member of the church where your father was an elder and his father before him. The tradition goes back six generations. You don't want to go against your family that way, my little girl. As you see, if you don't join with us, it will mean your brothers might eventually be lost to the church too."

To think that her indecision might keep Amos, Jakie and Johnny from joining the church alarmed Betsy. She was pleased that they were being trained in the Old Order at Uncle John's just as they would have been at home. Now she was afraid that her example would undo all that they had been taught. Would her going to college be a bad influence on the boys?

Betsy became confused and began to tremble when she realized how her actions affected those she loved. She wanted to run to her room to think it out by herself but Uncle John's deep-chested voice went on.

Betsy then asked, "Don't you believe there might be a time in a family when tradition changes as a new generation assumes a different attitude?" She had become curious to learn what the various denominations believed and practiced, and in which one she would feel most at home.

But Uncle John's face clouded as he said sternly, "You have confused your mind, girl, by reading too many worldly novels. I'm surprised at you!"

"Really, Uncle John, the novels I've read have helped me to understand life better, and I did what Mamma always advised about anything I enjoyed, to enjoy them to the glory of God."

"I guess your aunt Salina would agree with your mother about that. The really important things in the church to this family are the observances of the ordinances, baptism by immersion and the love-feast with its ordinance of feet-washing and the communion service. Remember that Jesus said to Peter that if He didn't wash his feet, he would have no part with Him. The serious thing here is that if we don't wash one another's feet, we too may have no part with Him."

"Uncle John, remember when Papa was conscious after his accident and I read Scripture to him? He was so disheartened and afraid he might not be saved. But just before he became unconscious, I heard him say in a whisper, 'Thy grace is sufficient.' "

"Oh yes, Betsy, I was so thankful to learn that. You know, of course, we Brethren believe salvation comes only from our Saviour's dying on the cross for us, but then we always stress that other important truth that 'faith without works is dead' and that we must be 'rich in good works.' I wish you would like our way of giving evidence by our dress that we belong to the kingdom of God and not to the world."

"Personally, Uncle John, I try to practice having the separation from the world as a thing experienced in what my heart is interested in and in the attitude of my mind."

"Oh Betsy, I do wish you would heed the separation from the world in respect to Dave O'Lear. You must believe me and judge that he's not a satisfactory young man for you to have as a friend. It's bad enough that he's not one of us, but he influenced my twins to give up their interest in the Old Order and I fear that he's influencing you in like manner."

"No, Uncle John, it would not be fair to put any blame on Dave, for he didn't say a single word about my not joining the Old Order."

"Well," Uncle John smiled a doubtful sort of smile, "when you have more experience with life, you'll see how easily a person is influenced by another and then maybe you'll come to understand that Dave did in fact influence you. But that's not the only reason I disapprove of him. It's best that you stay away because he'll never know how to make ends meet. When a boy rides around on a pony instead of getting down to work earning money, it's easy to see that he isn't thrifty. According to Old Order practice, it isn't right for you to be a friend to a man you aren't going to marry. Now, Betsy, I happen to think Paul Honstein is just right for a husband for you, and I do wish you would like him just as he likes you."

"Really, Uncle John, I'm not one bit interested in getting married."

After her conversation with Uncle John, Betsy had a chance

to tell Aunt Salina what they had talked about and mentioned Uncle John's objections to Dave.

"Exactly!" exclaimed Aunt Salina. "Your uncle is a good example of a person who'll never change his mind. He's been prejudiced against Dave ever since he got that pony. Well, I sometimes feel your uncle was turned against Dave because his pop bought the farm over there and made the house into a country home. But getting the pony for him was just too much, but he won't listen to me! One morning at family worship Pop was reading in Luke where the Saviour says 'a man's life consisteth not in the abundance of the things he possesses', but in 'having a soul that is rich toward God', and I said to Pop afterwards that that passage in Luke fits Dave better than any person I know in the Old Order."

"What did Uncle John say to that?"

" 'Ach,' he said, 'that just shows the women folk always gets mixed up when talking about religion.' "

"I can remember spending the day here when I was younger," Betsy related. "I used to watch the twins, Elias and James, playing with Dave. He was always so neat-looking and was mannerly and he spoke so clearly and well that I was really impressed with him. The three of them seemed inseparable whether they were playing ball or racing or exploring in the woods. And do you know, Aunt Salina, I was at a party in town once and I heard Dave play the piano. He plays so well!"

"Your uncle really became upset with himself because he allowed the twins to play with Dave. One day when Dave and Elias and James had earned some money in town they spent part of it buying candy and sitting in a pool room. Sooner than one might guess, word began circulating among Old Order families that Elder Butterbaugh's sons were playing pool, and when their father learned of it, he took a stand and forbade his sons to associate any more with Dave, whom he denounced as shiftless for inveigling his boys to participate in what was worldly!

"When the twins reached the age when they were expected to join the church," Aunt Salina continued, "as their older brother and sisters had done, they both insisted on putting off their decision. Uncle John felt baffled and declared to himself that Dave was to blame. After the twins were married and had settled down, Elias in Harrisburg and James in Chambersburg, they joined the Presbyterian Church instead of the Old Order. Your uncle John thinks that's proof enough of Dave's bad influence.

"When Uncle John challenged Dave about it, he admitted that the twins had inquired about the various churches in town, but he never suggested they should not become Old Order. Dave tried to win the favor of Uncle John but was always rebuffed, and more than once Uncle John lectured him on the need to give up his fondness for play and become a serious-minded worker. It seemed to make no difference that Dave was industrious in his studies and in helping his father at the printery. The old charge against him as a playboy riding on that pony was repeated over and over and even after he went away to school. Dave and Nick went away to the same school up there at Mercersburg, and Nick put the idea in Pop's head that Dave was a playboy at school. Today when Nick's a businessman in town, Pop thinks a heap of him. Pop likes to sit in his brother Zeke's store, and there Nick comes and sits down beside him. Pop is always full of praise for Nick when he comes home. But he doesn't seem to see how clever Nick is. After Nick says something in praise of Dave as if he and Dave were true friends, why then he says something that makes Pop think Dave isn't to be trusted at all."

Uncle John's plan to drive down to Aunt Mattie's to explain why Betsy ran away could not be carried out because of pressure at the moment from his farm work which forced him to postpone the trip from day to day. On Monday morning, one full week after Betsy had come to Uncle John's, she was dusting the sitting room when she heard a team coming up the lane and was startled to see it was Uncle Abe's. *This could mean trouble!* she exclaimed to herself. She heard Aunt Mattie accost Uncle John as he came down from the barn, "I felt certain you would come down the very next day and explain why you would support that ungrateful girl, and I'm so afraid you will let her go to college."

"Now, Mattie," responded Uncle John, "don't be so shrill! Let's go up to the house and talk this over sensibly."

"John, that's your cute way of trying to get out of trouble. You know you've done wrong to give Betsy a home. You should have brought her back that same Sunday afternoon!"

"Mattie, hush!" Uncle Abe was aroused. "John is an elder in the church and knows how to do as an elder, and his suggestion is not cute, but the only way to solve any trouble is by talking it over calmly. You won't accomplish anything by showing such fierce anger!"

Mattie kept quiet a minute as the three walked towards the steps to the porch, then she said, "John, I can't understand why you haven't said a word about being sorry that you did such an unchristian thing as to take Betsy in."

Uncle John stopped abruptly, "The girl has to have a home, Mattie, that's a Christian obligation, and I—."

"Yes, of course she needs a home! She had a home with us, but she was disobedient and ran away and you're just as guilty, John, for condoning what she did by taking her in!"

By this time they were on the porch and Betsy opened the door and said, "Aunt Mattie, I explained in my letter to you and Uncle Abe why I left your home."

"John," said Mattie sharply, "if we are to discuss this child's performance, she must be kept quiet and out of the room."

"All right, Aunt Mattie, I'll leave the room, but please remember that your constant scolding and mean criticism forced me to run away to Uncle John's." Then Betsy went down to the kitchen.

Aunt Salina was getting ready to hang a wash on the line, and Betsy offered to help. "No," Aunt Salina decided, "I won't hang the wash out now. We'll sit on the steps here and listen to what they say up there in the sitting room. Oh Betsy, I was afraid that Aunt Mattie would get so angry that she would almost explode."

They could hear Mattie declare she wanted the various congregations to know she had just one aim, to get Betsy to join the Old Order.

"She must be won by kindness and love," Uncle John retorted, "not by meanness and violence."

Mattie's voice was sharp. "I am never violent, John, and I wasn't mean, but I was simply being firm to do what any good Old Order member would do to get Betsy to join the church. Now you take her in and give her the comforts of your home and it's obvious that you have failed to do what an Old Order is supposed to do."

"No, Mattie, there is such a thing as acting according to love. Do you expect me to throw her out of my home? Since she has come back I've talked to her about joining the church, and I believe love will win her more surely than any other method."

"There is one thing certain, John, if she was in my home, she wouldn't get to college, for that's the surest way to get her never to become Old Order."

"Well, I'm her legal guardian and will send her to college because her father asked me to do that."

Mattie's voice became shrill, "You will find that the brethren and sisters in all the neighboring congregations will learn how you failed to do what an elder ought to do."

John was calm, "If I do what my conscience tells me to do, I'll be content."

Uncle Abe now spoke, "I can't tell you, John, how grieved I am that Mattie is so furious. The only thing to do is for the three of us to pray to God to dispose of this difficulty, and I suggest we now get down on our knees in prayer." So they knelt and Abe prayed that God would guide Betsy, and "each of us here shall leave the problem in Thy hands to be solved to Thy glory, Amen."

Then Uncle John prayed, "Lord, because we know God wants us to walk in love together, keep Satan from hindering us in serving Thee." When they got up again, Mattie was relentless, "Some day, John, you'll see that you are to blame for being so easy-going when you ought to be firm, but there's no use trying to change your mind once you've got it made up, so we'll go home."

John walked with Mattie and Abe to their buggy and said nothing more except good-bye.

After they had gone, Betsy thanked Uncle John for making clear to Aunt Mattie that he was providing a home for her. "Yes," he said, "but how unpleasant it is to have such fussing! The trouble is that Mattie knows she can get some of the brethren and sisters to side with her about this matter of you going to college. Are you certain, Betsy, in your heart that you ought to go to college this year?"

"Oh yes, Uncle John, I do want to get an education, but I hope you won't mind all this criticism."

"I am willing to stand the criticism if you are convinced you ought to go."

11

College Challenges

IT WAS ARRANGED for Betsy to go to the Brethren's Normal College, located at Huntingdon. But she began to be troubled again with doubts about the wisdom of this step as it concerned her brothers. Might it not be better for her to stay at home and look after their interests and possibly help them in planning their careers? Jakie was growing to be a tall, handsome boy and showed promise intellectually. But after talking it over with Aunt Salina, it was decided that Betsy should go to college now.

Since no one of her family had been to college, Betsy had vaguely thought of it as an extension of high school where the entire program was set and there were few choices to be made. But now she was in a different world; there were so many decisions to be made and so many procedures to be followed that she was at first pleasantly excited, then confused. It was in the chapel in Founders Hall that Betsy met various members of the faculty and especially her faculty adviser, but she felt hesitant about bothering him. However, he soon found her single-hearted interest in learning refreshing, and shortly her confusions were resolved and her program became clear to her.

Betsy's roommate, Mary Wills, was a girl from a neighboring town who came to college hoping to have lots of fun, and it wasn't long before she depended upon Betsy to help her, especially with getting papers written. Betsy and Mary were taking the same courses and when the time approached for a paper to be submitted, Mary was unconcerned whereas Betsy had hers ready to hand in. It wasn't until the night before the paper was due that Mary began to work and pleaded for help. Taking pity on her Betsy helped her to write the paper, but she was firm in telling Mary that it was her own responsibility. Betsy still occasionally helped her, but Mary gradually learned more self-discipline from Betsy's example and when she wrote to her family she told them that she had never known a country girl with such refinement, nor any girl with such a keen mind. She realized Betsy was a person to respect and admire, and in time she came to love her.

At college, Betsy was more free to enjoy the arts. To her delight, she was given a job as a waitress in the dining hall to earn extra money. That enabled her to take private piano lessons and gave her an opportunity to meet the music students.

Early in the term she received a letter from Mrs. O'Lear which was reassuring as she told her of the difficulties she herself had had in her first year at college and warned her of some of the discouragements she would encounter, but it ended on a cheerful note, "I know your adaptability and good sense will carry you over all these hurdles and you will be able to do your best work as you have always done." Mrs. O'Lear added that Dave had also had a trying experience at the university when he entered, and he sent a message that "the first weeks are the hardest, and don't let them get you down!"

Betsy appreciated Mrs. O'Lear's thoughtfulness so much that she wrote a reply immediately describing her program. She told of her courses in rhetoric, algebra, Latin, and the Bible. The course she talked about with the most enthusiasm was Latin in which they were studying Horace. Betsy became almost eloquent in telling Mrs. O'Lear that one could learn

from Horace how to be a truly cultivated person, by heeding
Horace's ideas on simplicity of living, and being steadfast,
and exercising a wise restraint, thereby observing the 'golden
mean.' Betsy had even memorized some of Horace's lyrics
which she enjoyed the most.

Betsy described to Mrs. O'Lear some of the most fascinating of the school activities. She especially liked the fellowship at the meals in the dining-room in the basement of
Founders Hall and she actually found it entertaining to
watch the distribution of the mail by the senior student at
the head of the table who would throw out the letters from
where he stood to the persons to whom they were addressed,
even if they were all the way across the room.

She told Mrs. O'Lear how she enjoyed being a member of
The Lyceum, the literary society of the college. Each Friday
evening the group met for debates, speeches, dramatic readings or programs of recitation. From time to time Betsy participated by reciting some of her favorite poems, but she
always enjoyed listening to the other students and talking
with them afterward.

Most of all, Betsy liked the daily chapel services in which
experienced preachers delivered a wide variety of helpful
messages.

Betsy confessed to Mrs. O'Lear that she was bewildered by
some of the views expressed by Dr. Baer, the professor of
Bible, who was beginning his second year of teaching. He
said that one need not experience any difficulty over the Bible
miracles, since they can be easily explained. Betsy had looked
forward with eager anticipation to the course in Bible. From
the time she was twelve years old she had begun reading in
the Bible each day according to the custom of everyone in
her Old Order home. By the time she finished high school
she had read through the Bible twice. At college she began
to read faithfully all the assigned readings in the course in
Bible, but too soon she was surprised, even shocked, at the
critics' handling of the Old Testament, and her professor's

doubtful remarks about miracles. She didn't want to complain to anyone. She asked herself if maybe she was a bit peculiar because of coming from an Old Order home. She tried to reason about her difficulty that possibly it wasn't as serious as she imagined it was, but she couldn't avoid being upset over such new and disturbing ideas. Keeping her dismay to herself became unsettling, and she decided to write again to Mrs. O'Lear.

"Dear Mrs. O'Lear, can you imagine what it was like for me to get the idea that the miracles recorded in the Bible did not necessarily happen as the Bible says? I cannot describe to you how this has shaken me! I was taught always to look upon the Bible as the absolute authority in the Christian faith and I have been disturbed also by an impression I got from some of the critics that the Pentateuch is hardly an inspired part of the Scripture but rather more or less a jumble of documents." Then she described to Mrs. O'Lear how she dealt with this problem. She read the Pentateuch again to see if it lacked unity, and read from it every day. When she finished it, she felt assured that it was a consistently connected whole. As she said to herself, *When one realizes that the Pentateuch teaches that man was created in the image of God, and gives the Ten Commandments and the Covenant, and teaches that we are to love God with all our heart and soul and to love our neighbor as ourself, and also that we are to meditate on God's word day and night, then one cannot help being impressed that it was inspired.*

Unfortunately she debated her problem too often at night when she should have been asleep. At the moment she was aware that her roommate was enjoying a sound sleep, Betsy was wishing she could sleep like that instead of tossing around on her bed. But she got some relief by quoting to herself passages from the psalms that she had long ago memorized: "Say among the heathen that the Lord reigneth," and "Know ye that the Lord he is God, it is He that hath made us and not we ourselves."

Betsy was learning about her new world by listening to the many and varied comments of her classmates. She was glad she liked being quiet instead of wanting to assert herself on every topic.

One Saturday afternoon, Betsy learned some new ideas while out walking with a senior. Henry Shank had remarked to his friends that he wanted to find out what sort of a girl Betsy was, "for she certainly is pretty and they say she has a keen mind." During a leisurely stroll he cautioned her about taking life too seriously. "We're going through this life only once, you know, and you might as well have a good time." He scoffed, "The college is making itself ridiculous in being so strict about drinking, and in expelling Jason Gibbs for being drunk downtown."

Betsy was shocked. "I fully approve of the college being strict about that. It's dreadful that students can even buy liquor downtown. My father taught me the psalm about wine 'making glad the heart of a man,' but my father was most emphatic that to get drunk was a mortal sin." She said her father in family worship used to quote Scripture as showing that man is 'accountable to a holy God for the deeds done in the body,' and that real happiness is possible only when a person 'walks by the Spirit.' "

Henry gave a sardonic laugh, "I wouldn't be surprised if young people someday refuse to take their fathers seriously."

Betsy's eyes flashed, "I respect the practice in the Old Order community where the young people are trained to have reverence in their hearts for God and to show honor to their parents."

Though they talked about other topics as they strolled back to the campus, Betsy suspected that she would not find Henry the sort of person to have for a friend, and decided she would not go out with him again.

Betsy received a reply from Mrs. O'Lear who said she had sent to Dave her letter and asked him to write her, "since he has the point of view of young people."

Dave's letter congratulated Betsy on being scholarly enough to read beyond what had been assigned. He advised her never to let any book disturb her that treats of great literature. "Just see what happened to the prestige of the higher criticism of Homer which only a few decades ago had gained such wide acceptance, and yet look at it today! The real need always is to be acquainted with the great literature itself. You have done the right thing in reading the Pentateuch again carefully. Don't become upset about what the critics say about the various documents. The important thing is to have made a careful acquaintance with the literaure, and yet it is interesting to know the views of the critics who can provide a scholarly introduction to the study of the Bible.

"I must tell you of a sermon I heard in Philadelphia by a distinguished Presbyterian minister who lamented that too many today, including ministers, 'think desperately low of God,' and in his sermon and prayer this minister showed that he thought 'high' of God. He declared that when one recognizes that God is 'He Who Is,' the eternally Existing One, who is an infinite 'ocean of existence,' one has no difficulty with miracles, but when one thinks 'low' of God, then he doesn't really have a God and has to explain miracles away on purely natural grounds. He made a remarkable comment on the devotion to science seen in various quarters today. As he said, 'Science reveals to us the laws according to which change happens in the world. What science cannot reveal to us is why this world, with its laws, its order, and its intelligibility exists.' Then he said, 'Man cannot live by bread alone but by every Word of God,' 'Seeing He Himself giveth to all life, and breath, and all things.'"

At the close of his letter Dave added, "Let me warn you about a weakness in teachers of wanting the students to parrot back to them their favorite views and interpretations. Not all teachers are guilty of this, of course, for there are genuine scholars of integrity, but the average run of teachers find it very tempting to engage in their favorite propaganda!

Take such with a grain of salt. By all means, Betsy, ask your instructor for a private conference and discuss the whole problem with him."

Then Dave expressed the hope that Betsy was making progress on the piano, and he hoped to hear her play something when he came to call on her.

When she wrote to him she thanked him for his very helpful letter "which will stimulate me to grow intellectually, and I appreciate the fact that you who are so much more widely read in contemporary literature than I am, are a convinced believer." She reflected that his grandfather had been the most influential preacher and elder in the Dunker Church in Waynesboro and had also been a success in business.

At the close of her letter she mentioned the great interest she was taking in practicing on the piano, and thanked him for his encouragement. She could not help but add that she would always be glad to see him.

After Betsy wrote to Dave she decided to act on his advice about having a conference with her professor. After hesitating for several days, Betsy calmed her fears that she might say the wrong thing to Dr. Baer and finally requested a conference with him. He replied that he would be happy to see her that afternoon.

All that day Betsy couldn't heep her mind off the conference and tried to arrange in order the various points she wanted to make, but sighed to herself how poorly equipped her mind was! As she walked to Dr. Baer's office she recalled how her mother used to counsel her after she had had a discussion with her father that she ought always to listen carefully to what the other person says and always be fair-minded and clear in the reasons she gave in reply. She hoped she had learned how to conduct a discussion.

Dr. Baer was a minister of the Dunker Church, now in his forties, and had been on the faculty for just one year. He enjoyed unusual prestige in the college community because he had done graduate study abroad, having studied in Berlin and

Göttingen. As he was cordial in welcoming Betsy, she was encouraged to tell him at once what troubled her. The controversial ideas had been put forth in a book listed in the recommended readings. She mentioned the title.

"Ah, yes, I admit that is not a milk diet," he smiled.

"But Dr. Baer, do you think it's a 'diet' at all, for doesn't it tear down instead of building up?"

"It is necessary, Miss Brecher, for an educated person to know all about the critical examination of the biblical documents."

"I do want to be educated, sir, but isn't it possible and even logical to have a valid questioning about the attitude of the critics?"

"In maturing, a young person passes from the juvenile period when he blindly accepts whatever he reads, to the critical period when he questions everything. He will then begin to work out his faith on critical principles."

Betsy asked, "Suppose that deep down within a person's soul there is a love for the Word of God and a desire to heed the word, is it good for him to pay attention to a critic who doesn't believe that the Holy Scripture is inspired of God?"

"In this course one is dealing with something like a cross-section of humanity, many of whom today are enamored with science, and in dealing with such a group, one should learn how to take the Bible seriously without necessarily taking it literally."

"But isn't there a danger, Dr. Baer, of looking upon God too lightly if one gets into the attitude of questioning the Scriptures? Some of the students have even mentioned that they believe God is an idea that man has fabricated for the sake of convenience."

"Ah, yes," smiled Dr. Baer, "there is no one so fond of being skeptical as an adolescent, but as he grows older he then looks back upon his skeptical assertions as being very immature!"

"I am sorry to admit," Betsy added, "that since I began

reading the critics I have been bothered at times by a questioning attitude about prayer. "I have actually asked myself if prayer does anything more than provide a benefit to my own mind as the result of a refreshing mental exercise, instead of realizing that I am actually in touch with the God of Abraham, of Isaac, and of Jacob. May I tell you of an experience I had, sir?"

"Yes, certainly, Miss Brecher. I enjoy talking to a student who is in earnest."

"In our Old Order home it was our practice for each person to read from the Bible every day. While I was in high school I met a lovely lady in Waynesboro who gave me a number of religious tracts by English writers, and she talked to me several times about those tracts and said how important it was to be guided by the Bible as the Word of God."

"Yes, Miss Brecher, that may be a helpful attitude for you, but what about all those young people who think only in terms of the scientific? Those who are trained in biology and physics and the other sciences have a questioning in their minds that the writers of Scripture, who wrote these documents in a pre-scientific age, did not understand nature scientifically."

Betsy looked puzzled, then she said, "I think I see your point, but don't you think that if one stresses unduly the human element in the writing of Scripture, he tends to overlook the specific claim of Scripture that it was inspired by the Holy Spirit and is authoritative for our salvation? One of the tracts that the lady gave me said, 'the Bible will keep you from sin, or sin will keep you from the Bible.' Don't you think students should realize that the Bible teaches that all men have sinned against God and need forgiveness and redemption?"

"Well," said Dr. Baer, as he stood up, "It's a very complicated problem dealing with such a great variety of young people."

"Yes, of course, Dr. Baer, but shouldn't young people understand that the Bible claims it is inspired and speaks with authority about our relationship to God and is different from any other book? You remember, Professor Baer, how the Apostle Paul speaks of 'the holy scriptures which are able to make thee wise unto salvation.' "

"Well, yes, to be sure," he said as he shook hands with her. "Thanks for calling on me, and always feel free to come to see me."

Betsy thanked the professor for his kindness. As she walked back to her hall, she was pleased she had mentioned certain points that were of prime importance. She felt she had gained one thing; she would now feel free to go to Dr. Baer with questions at the close of his lectures, because he showed he was interested in young people and wanted to help them. But as she thought it over she began to feel uneasily that Dr. Baer had not really answered her questions. She went over the conversation again and again and began to question whether she had fully understood him. She didn't feel like studying and for quite a while that evening gave herself up to reverie. She saw herself during her years in high school when she read in the Bible every day. *In those days I looked upon the Bible as true from beginning to end, and I loved it, and I still do!*

A few days later Betsy was not a little surprised to receive a letter from Nick Mellers at Waynesboro asking if he might come to see her. She explained in her reply that most of her leisure time was taken up with doing the numerous assignments in reading, and she could not afford the time to see him.

Although Betsy hoped it was wise of her to put an end to Nick's endeavors to see her, she became aware that she was easily perplexed; it was difficult to free herself from an inner tension. Whenever she enjoyed a party at the college she found herself the next morning wondering if her enjoyment of the party was not a little on the worldly side. She was especially critical of herself for being jealous at a party one evening when Roger, who was her escort, made a fuss over Marjorie. She was perturbed with herself, too, for wondering if she were as attractive as Marjorie. She said to herself the next day that if she couldn't enjoy a party without making odious comparisons and becoming jealous, she was being downright worldly-minded and ought to discipline herself. She began to think seriously about the problem of pleasures at college and reasoned that if she were to enjoy the contacts with the boys at the parties and not permit herself to feel jealous or slighted, it might help to make her a more likable personality. She participated in the socials after that and found she enjoyed them more.

Dave had written that he wanted to come to see Betsy and she felt that Dave would so manage his visit that it would not interfere with her studies or his own. He came on the morning train, had dinner with Betsy at the college and took a walk with her over the campus. He asked about her courses of study and encouraged her in her work. Then he returned to Philadelphia early that evening on the train. In this way he found he could make a number of visits without interfering too much with Betsy's work or his own.

Betsy's first interest was always in her studies. After making honor grades in her mid-year exams she was beginning to be launched upon her new semester's work, when in February a visiting preacher of the Dunker Church in Virginia came to conduct a series of meetings in the college chapel. He was tall and well-built and wore a long brown beard that tapered to a point, which reminded Betsy of her father. When she went to hear him preach, this too reminded her of her father. She talked to him afterwards and revealed her Old Order connections, but to her surprise he reminded her that "we are all Dunkers, just as the Old Order members are," and he explained that "the important thing is for you to be baptized and to realize you are a member of the church which the Scripture speaks of as the bride of Christ."

Betsy tried to be severely logical in reflecting on this problem but she couldn't avoid being guided by her moods. After talking with the minister from Virginia she felt she ought to join the church at the college, but when she speculated what Uncle John would say, she came to a conclusion that such an important step ought to be postponed until a later time.

But still her mind was confused and she was agitated even after going to bed. *If Uncle John will not approve of my joining the college church, will I be willing to join the Old Order? But ach! I have so many reasons to hesitate joining the Old Order.*

Betsy pulled the sheet over her face and closed her eyes. She saw again the service she attended with Doris in the Presbyterian church. *What a remarkable sermon that was! I remember how childish I was in thinking the preacher was speaking directly to me, for he was dealing with problems that do indeed trouble the Old Order.* She thought again of that text, "All things are yours," and that the preacher said that if you submit unto God your various interests, He will bless those interests that He designs for your own good. She was so perplexed, she couldn't reason or think straight, but she understood clearly enough that she would never be able to feel at home in the Old Order church.

After the special meetings were over and she got down to intensive study, she became interested in her new courses, especially an introductory course to medieval civilization. After a few weeks of enjoying her studies she asked herself if perhaps she had an inborn desire to participate in the cultivated life of literature and art and music. Enjoying art and literature was not worldly according to the Dunker minister who had spoken at the college, but it would certainly be so regarded by the presiding elder of the Old Order!

12

Future Plans

A HIGHLIGHT of Betsy's spring vacation was the walk along the lane and up the hill behind the farm because she met Dave on the way. He had come home for the weekend and they both enjoyed the unexpected opportunity to talk. Dave told of some of his college experiences and then he asked Betsy how she was dealing with her difficulties about the Bible. She agreed with the comment from his letter that one must always think highly of God.

At the end of their walk, they went to Dave's house where he played Mozart's Piano Sonata in C Major. Of course, Dave was interested in the progress of Betsy's lessons, so she played several short pieces she had learned. He was so pleased that he asked her to sing. Betsy was a member of the college choir and had learned several new songs. Mrs. O'Lear, unable to resist the music, had come to listen. Then she served tea and doughnuts and the three of them spent the remainder of the afternoon talking about college life.

The following school year, Dave's father suffered a severe heart attack. He could no longer manage his printing business, so Dave quit his job in the law office in Philadelphia and returned home to take his father's place. It was difficult for Dave to make the adjustment from the city to the country and from an interesting office to a business which he felt was

not the least bit stimulating. Because train service from
Waynesboro was poor, Dave was additionally frustrated because he could see Betsy only when she came home for vacation. The two corresponded more and more frequently, providing mutual encouragement.

Each year at the college was a treat for Betsy, and she was
surprised how quickly the time passed. She spent her sum-
mers with Aunt Salina, helping her in all her work, but now
she ventured over to Dave's home from time to time to practice on the piano.

When Betsy returned home during the spring vacation of
senior year, Uncle John said he and Aunt Salina would like
to talk with her about her future plans, and he suggested it
was time now to decide about the man to be her husband.

"Oh, dear Uncle John," Betsy laughed, "do you know I
don't feel the least bit of interest in getting a husband!"

"It isn't important how you feel, Betsy." Uncle John said
soberly. "Choosing a husband for you is a practical matter
for your parents, and now your guardian, to be concerned
about. Of course, we want you to marry a fine young man
who has money."

Betsy looked startled. "Isn't this placing too much value
on money, Uncle John?"

"Ach, no Betsy! How can you get along in this world without money, I'd like to know! So many people aren't thrifty
any more, but they just spend and spend and spend! You certainly want a husband who is thrifty and financially established. Now as you know, I have Paul in mind for you; he
knows how to earn money. He's been buying up houses and
repairing them himself, making them over to look like new
and then selling them at a fine profit, and he knows how to
invest his money wisely. He now owns four houses that he
rents and is really getting a good income. In fact, Betsy, I
don't know who else I could approve who would be as fine a
husband for you as Paul."

"Now really, Uncle John, as I've said before, I'm not one bit interested in getting married."

"John, Betsy will know it is time for her to marry when she falls in love," Aunt Salina commented in her sweet way.

"Marriage is an important matter, Salina. It must be carefully considered and planned, not 'fallen into.' The more I think of Paul, the more certain I am that he'd make an excellent husband for Betsy."

"Yes, Uncle John, I'll be glad to consider Paul whenever I begin to think seriously of marriage."

"If you don't want to get married now, Betsy, how do you plan to earn money?"

"Papa allowed me to go to college so that I could teach and support myself. I plan to apply for a position in Waynesboro as a high school teacher."

Betsy's college commencement was a gala experience for her. She was proud to have her brothers, Jakie and Johnny, present as her guests when she was awarded a prize for literary excellence. At the close of the exercises as the members of the graduating class emerged from the chapel in Founders Hall they collected in groups or wandered over the lovely campus. Betsy walked with her brothers to where the president of the college stood in a group, and she thanked him for what the college had done for her. Both Jakie and Johnny had decided that they were interested in a college education, too. The president remarked, "You know, there is never any question about the character of the young people who come from an Old Order home." Then he shook hands with the boys, "You will be very welcome here." He added that the college community would miss Betsy greatly. This attention the president paid to Betsy and her brothers pleased each of them.

Upon their return home from the college, Betsy began looking for an opportunity to talk to Uncle John about Jakie going to college. She knew how strenuously he would object.

But Jakie wanted to go to college. He had grown tall and strong from his work on the farm, but he was also one of the finest students in his senior class.

One rainy evening, Betsy found Uncle John relaxed. She began, "Now that Jakie is eighteen and completing high school, don't you think we ought to consider what he might want to take up in the future and especially any plan for his going to college?"

At the mention of college for Jakie, Uncle John's face became red as he energetically got up from his chair, like a rooster bristling up his crest, and declared, "No, Miss, you aren't going to take away my boy Jakie. Why, he's the best farmer I know! How could college help him?" he said with a snort. "He'll make enough at farming, and besides, he likes the Old Order now but college could lead him astray." Uncle John was red in the face and took time to catch a breath, then continued vigorously, "I have never seen a boy show such a knack for knowing the right thing to do in any predicament in farming. He'll be an honor to his pop in being as good a farmer as he was, and he'll take over his pop's farm and he'll be well fixed for life."

"Yes, Uncle John, I'm glad Jakie is highly efficient in farmign, but he might be just as efficient in any other work, say, as a chemist. He told me he would like to go to college to study science."

"Ach, no, Betsy, that's a foolish notion a body gets at high school. But after he comes to his senses he'll know that isn't what he ought to do."

Betsy asked Uncle John to talk to Jakie about his plans. "Judging from what Jakie said to me, he has become greatly interested in chemistry and would like to get college training; he knows there are a number of good positions available to someone with a college degree."

"Ach, Betsy, I'm shocked at you, honestly! Why in the world would you disturb an old man whose heart's been set on having the boy follow in your pop's and my footsteps and take over the farm?"

"Well, really, Uncle John, why wouldn't it be good to help a child do what he has a talent for and not try to impose your plans upon him?"

"Betsy, such new fangled ideas could be the ruin of our people! What is needed is to take a firm stand for what we know is the right way."

"Uncle John, I'm going to say to you what my mother said to me—'pray about it.' What would the Lord want Jakie to do?"

"All right, Betsy, that's the proper way, of course, but don't try to influence him yourself."

Jakie made out a good case for going to college when Uncle John talked to him. He showed a concern for the farms but felt there were advantages for him at college that he should not miss. Though Uncle John was not convinced, Betsy and Jakie worked out a plan, by which Jakie would earn money by getting a job in town during the following year. As Betsy would be teaching, she would be able by next year to borrow the money to pay for Jakie's first year at college.

On the day of Betsy's commencement, Dave's father had died suddenly. It was a shock and disappointment to everyone. Dave decided to continue working at the printing business and allow his older brother, Raymond, to continue farming. Dave abandoned his plans for a career in law but he hoped that the print shop might be an opportunity for him to become established as a writer.

The next time Betsy saw Dave at the town library she told him that she had been chosen to teach at Waynesboro high school.

"But, Betsy, where will you live? I hope you don't plan to stay at your Uncle John's! You would never be able to practice your music. You ought to engage a room in some home in town which has a piano on which you'd be free to practice every day."

She was pleased with his suggestion. "Why yes, of course, Dave," she replied, "you are certainly right, and I wish you would recommend such a home."

Dave promised he would make an inquiry. Within a few days he told her of the choice home of a Norwegian family who were fond of music and who would be glad to let Betsy have a room and the use of their piano. Betsy's face immediately lighted up.

The owner of the house, Hans Nilsen, was reared in Oslo and was now the chief draftsman at the Flanders Machine Company in town. Dave said his friends looked upon Hans as something of an artist in playing the violin. Dave had played the piano in his home when they had played trios, for Mrs. Nilsen, who was also from Norway, played the cello. Betsy recalled having met Mrs. Nilsen at tea at Doris's.

"You are certainly helpful, Dave, in finding this home for me, and I'm sure Aunt Salina will be pleased."

Even Uncle John seemed to think that Betsy had done well to get into such a good home. For a graduation gift, he gave her a horse and buggy. He added, however, that she should be wary of Dave's friendship and he made it quite clear that he would never approve of Dave as a husband.

"Oh, Uncle John," laughed Betsy, "I'm really not interested in getting married. I enjoy having a friendship with Dave but that doesn't say we want to fall in love."

"Ah yes, my little girl," he smiled, "but that's the way things usually go, and I wouldn't want to hurt you later on if you should fall in love with him, for you should realize I could not approve of him." Then he tried to explain why. "In the first place, he isn't thrifty, and his dad was not the thrifty kind, but a spender. When his boy should have been earning money, what was he doing? Why, riding on a pony! In the second place, he's head over heels in debt at his printery. He just isn't the sort who'll ever become financially established. In the third place, he made himself an outsider years ago when he set the twins against joining the Old Order."

"Please excuse me, Uncle John, but I asked Dave about his influence on the twins, and he declared he never suggested they should not become Old Order."

"Ah yes, Betsy, that's the way the world explains facts away. But actually if it hadn't been for Dave, the twins today would be Old Order, and I could never agree to such a person marrying into our family."

"As I said, Uncle John, I'm not thinking of Dave as a husband, but really, it would be a great help to me to have him as a friend and to practice on his piano at times."

"Well, you may be right," he added. "Since you're a sensible girl, I'm going to trust your judgment. But I want you to remember what I said about him."

"I doubt very much if I'll ever have to cross that bridge," she smiled.

Mrs. O'Lear and Dave were pleased to have Betsy come and practice on their piano, which she did often. On Saturdays when Dave sometimes was home and liked to have a conversation with Betsy, she would not hesitate to slight the practicing. One day she asked a question about his private affairs. "Uncle John is still very critical of you. He has the idea that you're head over heels in debt. Where would he get such information, or does he imagine these things?"

"I've seen your Uncle John in Zeke's store quite often talking with Nick Mellers who knows all about my financial affairs. You see, my father asked me to renovate the printery. Nick provided some helpful advice on how to make the shop more modern, but it cost a lot of money, so Nick supported a large loan. It was a worthwhile investment, but it was expensive. I've been working in the shop since I was twelve years old and I know how difficult the machinery was to run. One of the presses had been in use since my great-grandfather started this business in 1865!"

"Dave, did you say you'd been helping in the shop since you were twelve?"

"Sure, Raymond's chores were on the farm, mine were in the printery."

"I guess Uncle John doesn't know about that! He's always critical that you were out riding a pony when you should have been earning money."

"This is what you find with some of these 'old-timers'—their prejudice keeps them from recognizing facts. I told him plainly of working at the printery for my father. Anyway, Nick was really helpful in devising ways to iron out some of the problems in the shop. He's like a partner in the business. He has one of the keenest minds in town for business."

Betsy was busy at Aunt Salina's every day of the summer, sewing, helping in the work of the home, practicing on the piano over at Dave's, and reading the books she got at the town library. She spent as much time with her brothers as she could; they idolized her. Jakie had a job as a reporter on the local paper and he found it helpful to consult Betsy and Laura frequently about handling the news writing.

Betsy drove her new horse and carriage to visit Aunt Mattie. While she was in college, she wrote to her aunt frequently and Mattie softened somewhat when she realized that college was not as harmful as she feared it might be.

Aunt Mattie was especially pleased when Betsy inquired about Paul Honstein. "Well now, Betsy," said Aunt Mattie becoming more lively, "You just ought to see what a fine-looking man Paul has become. He's not only taller than ever, but since you were here, he's been doing such a lot of studying to make a man out of himself and you'll like talking to him, I know!"

"Yes," replied Betsy, "I shall enjoy seeing Paul again."

"That's a good girl! Why don't you come for supper on Friday and I'll invite Paul." Betsy graciously accepted.

When Paul came, Betsy was indeed surprised, despite all that Aunt Mattie had said about his looks. She saw that he was now a handsome young man, and more importantly he had a gentle manner. It amazed her that he could sit quietly and talk almost with ease. He wanted to talk about the reading which he pursued because of Betsy's urgings. He said he read in the Bible every day and was memorizing some favorite psalms. A high school teacher whom he had met interested him in some adventure stories by Mark Twain and other prominent American authors. Betsy congratulated Paul on his reading because he had clearly increased in understanding and his interests had expanded beyond the realm of farming.

When he was ready to leave, Paul asked Betsy if he might see her again. She said she didn't know when she might be down to Aunt Mattie's again, but she'd be glad to see him at Uncle John's if he cared to come. Paul left Aunt Mattie's much happier than when he had come.

During the summer months Nick Mellers called on Betsy a number of times and Uncle John observed to his wife, "I certainly prefer Nick to Dave as a friend of Betsy's. I'm afraid Dave will always be something of a failure in money matters." Betsy felt that Nick tried to be lively and entertaining so she would enjoy his company. He wanted her to go with him to the tavern in town for dinner but she declined with thanks.

13

Woodwinds

DAVE TOOK BETSY out to the country home of the Nilsens where she was welcomed as if she were an old friend. Their house was a large colonial style frame house a few miles north of town in a grove of oaks, beeches, and maples in ten acres of woodland, which the Nilsens named Woodwinds. Hans said he thought Betsy would enjoy the wild flowers, especially the lady slippers that flourished in the rich soil up on the ridge. Betsy was given a room on the top floor which enjoyed sunshine all day long, but what really impressed her was the grand piano in the music room which she was free to play at any time. She thanked the Nilsens for taking her in and thanked Dave for suggesting the arrangement.

It seemed a great adventure to Betsy as she moved out to Woodwinds. Hans Nilsen was a solid person with a beautiful head of air, ash blond, a full face, clean shaven, a ruddy complexion, and deep-set blue eyes that looked out upon the world with tolerance and a genial sense of fun. He had come to this country from Norway as a young man; he had studied at the University, and now was established in one of the main firms in town.

His wife, Karin, had been reared in Oslo. She, too, was gifted in music, playing the cello with even greater artistry than the piano. She was tall and distinguished-looking like her husband, sturdy and a bit portly. Her face was full, her blue eyes animated. She had an eager mind and was charged with an energy that made her an undoubted leader in her numerous activities. She was one of the wisest of mothers, and being naturally fond of people, she was a popular hostess. The Nilsens had two married sons, one in Minnesota and the other in Michigan.

Betsy from the first enjoyed her fellowship with Mr. and Mrs. Nilsen. They made her feel a part of the family when every evening they were home they asked her to join them in playing trios. After a time she made some new friendships in town and renewed her friendship with Doris who was now Mrs. Benchoff, and Ethel in whose home she was entertained with a number of other girls from her high school class. But her greatest treat was in going out to Uncle John's and having quiet fellowship with Aunt Salina.

When Betsy began her new career as a teacher, she remembered how she had always admired her high school English teacher was was now teaching in a college in Illinois, and she wanted to be as helpful and stimulating as he. One of her best students in the sophomore class was a black girl named Louise who told Betsy how much time she spent in practicing on the piano. From time to time Betsy asked her to come out to Woodwinds in the afternoon where they played duets. Betsy was always pleased when students came to her classroom after school to discuss problems, too. She made them feel welcome and took plenty of time to give them satisfaction. There was one week when she met young people in her classroom every day to help them with their studies or sometimes to discuss personal problems.

Even though Betsy had no idle moments, she was shocked to find she still had to contend with a conscience that accused her of being disrespectful to her parents. At times she would walk or drive from the school to Woodwinds at the close of the day's session, trying to reason about her girlhood performance in her home, but her reason was often too fragile to grapple with emotional onslaughts. She saw herself as ungrateful, and lacking an appreciation of the quiet virtues of the Old Order. By the time she reached Woodwinds she was often depressed, but she always found a pleasant release by playing some of her favorite pieces by Schubert, Schumann and Mozart. She worked hard on Mozart's Piano Sonata in C Major, hoping to be able to play it well enough to win Dave's approval.

Betsy sometimes would drop in at Laura's apartment and always came away smiling. Sidney, Jr., four years old, and Rebecca, not quite two, thought Aunt Betsy the best of playmates and wanted her to come in every day! It was good to talk to Laura, too, because of a new closeness the sisters felt after the death of their parents.

Laura told Betsy how happy she was in the Episcopal Church.

"Oh, I'm so glad," beamed Betsy. "If you like the liturgy, I don't see how anyone could improve on the Episcopal service! I went to the Episcopal church a number of times while I was at college. The atmosphere was very worshipful. I can't tell you how glad I am that you feel at home there.

"Laura, you know," Betsy confided, "for some time now I've been disturbed because I didn't honor Mama and Papa as I should have."

But Laura boomed, "If you are troubled, then I ought to be in torment since I was actually disrespectful to our parents while you were always considerate of them. I've realized since that I should have been more thoughtful. I've prayed for forgiveness, though. You should do the same. Claim God's forgiveness and go on from there, Betsy. Don't let your mind be continually troubled by past regrets."

Betsy thanked Laura for her sisterly advice and decided to heed what she had said.

One day in March Mrs. Nilsen was surprised to see a patriarchal personage walking up their lane. She judged from Betsy's description of her uncle who he was and she was curious to meet him. He wore a broad brimmed black hat and an overcoat, and *What a magnificent beard!* she exclaimed to herself. Though he was hesitant about coming in, Mrs. Nilsen succeeded in getting him to sit down in the living room.

"I stopped by, Mrs. Nilsen, to ask you to tell Betsy that her Aunt Salina and I would be pleased if she would come for a visit next weekend," he began.

"I'll certainly tell her. You know, my husband and I are so fond of Betsy."

"Yes," he replied with satisfaction, "she's a good girl."

"We're so proud of the progress she's made at the piano. She gives to my husband and me the impression of being something of an artist."

"She always has been persistent at anything she was interested in. Have you learned how they like her as a teacher?"

Mrs. Nilsen's eyes danced, "You will be pleased to learn that the principal of the high school is full of praise of Betsy as a teacher. My husband and he are friends and he spoke to Hans that Betsy is a credit to the school."

After a short, polite discussion of farming and business at the Flander's Machine Company, in which Uncle John owned stock, John Butterbaugh returned home with a high opinion of the Nilsen family.

Betsy was thrilled with Uncle John's invitation. She loved the farm in the early spring and the simple charm of the Old Order home.

When a few days later Uncle John saw Betsy's buggy coming up the lane, he came down from the house to welcome her, and said it was good of her to come. After kissing Aunt Salina Betsy ran down the porch steps and out into the yard looking around eagerly, exclaiming that everything was just as lovely as she had imagined it! She knew that Aunt Salina would take advantage of the recent dry spell to have her garden freshly spaded, "and just see the onions beginning to peep through the ground. And over there the crocuses and the daffodils are helping us welcome spring! How lovely it is here!" Then she told of the flowers blooming in Hans's rock garden.

Aunt Salina, Betsy, and Uncle John were talking in the sitting room when Ann came and shortly Johnny and Amos rushed in. They made Betsy very welcome. Ann went down to the kitchen and prepared some refreshment for Betsy and the boys—fresh apple pie covered with rich cream.

Ann said she had just returned from a call at the O'Lears', and she indiscreetly mentioned, "Dave was there and was pleased to learn you were coming for a visit." At the mention of Dave's name, Uncle John's eyes opened wide. He had been rocking gently in his ladder-back chair but now he sat motionless.

"Ach, my dear little girl, now that does indeed disappoint me, to know Dave is so interested." Uncle John began in a grandfatherly tone of voice but towards the end it was more like a magisterial tone. "As I have often informed you, I could not approve of him as a husband for you. Your Aunt Mattie once said I don't scold you sharp enough. I told her that a smart girl like Betsy did not need to be scolded so much as reasoned with. I hope you don't prove me wrong." Then he added earnestly, "You must remember I have a very great responsibility as your guardian and must consider everything that has to do with a suitable husband for you."

Aunt Salina could keep quiet no longer and stopped rocking her chair, "Now Pop, you want to remember Betsy's young, and don't forget that you were young once, too. Don't forget about the time you came to see me at my pop's and he wouldn't leave you come inside because he said you'd never amount to anything and were a failure on your own pop's farm, and don't you remember how you got with me at church the next Sunday after preaching was over and we talked out in the yard while the elders were still having a meeting inside."

Aunt Salina, Betsy, and Ann and the boys laughed heartily

at this vigorous recital of Uncle John's efforts as a lover, and he, too, joined in the laughter. "There's no use trying to contend against the women folk! Well, I'm thankful, Mom, it all worked out so good." Aunt Salina's happy recollection dispelled the tension and brightened the room like the appearance of sunshine after a storm. Then Uncle John explained that Paul Honstein was coming for a little visit and would be there for supper.

"Well, that will be pleasant!" Betsy said, and added that the last time she was with Paul they had had a very pleasant conversation.

"Yes, Betsy dear, that's a good girl!" Uncle John's eyes were shining.

Betsy wished Uncle John would realize that she could enjoy talking to Paul but she also enjoyed Dave and Nick, "and I don't think about falling in love with any of them, and I do wish you wouldn't be afraid whenever any mention is made of Dave."

"Well, well," he smiled, "as I've said to you before, I feel I ought to warn you so you won't forget that I could never approve of Dave."

Paul drove up the lane while Uncle John was talking. They went down the steps to welcome him, and Paul's face was full of blushes as Betsy shook hands with him. After talking with the family, Paul and Betsy sat out on the porch and he asked her to read aloud from some books she recommended, especially some poetry. She read from Longfellow's *Evangeline* and parts of *The Song of Hiawatha,* and Paul showed a real interest in her reading.

During the summer Betsy was concerned about getting the money to pay for her brother Jakie's first year at college. She learned of a retired businessman in town who often made loans to deserving people, and she was pleased to find that he regarded her as deserving. He agreed to make the loan she needed.

When Jakie entered college in September he was from the

first an energetic student. He wrote enthusiastically about his studies and his splendid professor in chemistry. He closed almost every letter by thanking Betsy for helping him to get to college. When she wrote to him, she tried to encourage him just as Dave and Mrs. O'Lear had helped her.

14

The Rivalry

NICK PHONED BETSY frequently but she wondered if perhaps it would be better to tell him she was not interested in having him as a friend. She always declined his invitation to go to the tavern for dinner.

On a Friday afternoon in March when spring was in the air, Betsy was walking home feeling fatigued after strenuous hours of teaching. Her feet were burning as if she had been walking on a desert's burning sand. But when she reached Woodwinds, she laughed at finding the fatigue all gone like the sudden disappearance of the moon under a cloud. To be welcomed by Peggotty, the collie, as she came springing through the air from the walled terrace beyond the house, which Betsy called "Peg's Perch," then to loiter down the stone path under the giant oaks, was as refreshing to her as swimming in the pond last summer. As she passed Hans's rock garden now once again showing itself as the snow gradually disappeared, she imagined the tulips and columbine that would be there within a month or two.

When she entered the hallway, Trofast, the Shetland Island sheep dog, rushed pell-mell down the steps to welcome her home. She decided to go up to her room and rest a bit before Karin was ready to serve tea. But Trofast's tail was wagging so vigorously she realized she must pay attention to him. She took time to caress Romulus and Remus, the twin kittens now regarded as her own pets, and so eager were they for Betsy's attention that they blocked her way as she went up the stairs. As she stretched out on the spool daybed in her room she was almost asleep, when she heard a tap on the door and was disappointed to learn that a caller awaited her in the living room. When Karin revealed it was Nick Mellers, Betsy was annoyed. "Why, he's become extremely self-assured! He didn't even phone to ask if he might come!" As Karin looked perplexed, Betsy tried to explain about her attitude towards Nick. "Nick is handsome and understandably popular with the girls, but we have almost no common interests. Oh well, he's here now, so I'll freshen up and go down to meet him."

As Betsy entered the living room, Nick rose, and in apologizing for coming without phoning he expressed concern over her becoming too much engrossed in her work, and thought he might provide a pleasant relaxation for her after the strain of teaching and trying to resolve the difficulties of students without making her feel there were any engagements to be kept. Such sentiments were disarming, like the warm breezes of this March thaw melting the snow.

Betsy forgot her irritation over Nick's impromptu visit and within five minutes she was enjoying his company. After a short period of conversation about Nick's sister Dorothy, Nick suggested, "Why don't we continue our visit over dinner at the tavern?"

Once again, Betsy politely refused the invitation.

"Come Betsy, you ought to enjoy life a bit and have a good time once in a while."

"Oh, but Nick, I do enjoy life so much living quietly here at Woodwinds surrounded by art, literature, and music."

Just then, Karin came into the room and, sensing the tension from Betsy's refusal to dine at the tavern, she invited Nick to have dinner with them. They enjoyed a delicious dinner and afterwards Nick was given a sample of the lovely music which Betsy enjoyed with the Nilsens almost every evening. Nick expressed his appreciation of Betsy's musical talents, but he frankly admitted that the music seemed too dainty for him; it seemed to lack masculinity.

Hans and Nick played a game of billiards, and Hans was surprised at Nick's skill; then there was more talk as the four of them sat in the music room. After Nick left them, Hans remarked as he lit his pipe that Nick undoubtedly made a splendid appearance and in some of his talk lived up to that impression, "but what a pity about his taste in music! And what a pity that he is so engrossed in making money! That seems to be the one thing he's vitally interested in. I tried to get him to talk about music but each time he turned the conversation back to his business deals. I've read items in the local paper about Nick and I've heard a good deal of talk about him but I never talked to him before. I can't say I'm too favorably impressed. He has much in his favor. He's a man's man and likes people and he likes the girls—as his fondness for Betsy indicates, but he's dominated by such a terrific drive to make money. I can understand, Betsy, why you haven't encouraged him to come often."

Betsy looked serious, "Nick can engage very well in idle conversation but his real weakness lies in being worldly-minded; that is, he has no vital interest in art or music or literature or religion, just an interest in gadgets that attract attention and an inordinate value placed on money and social status. I'm sometimes tempted to feel that Nick's soul is almost bankrupt."

Hans laughed, "I think you've hit the nail on the head! It interests me to observe that though Dave doesn't make the exciting personal appearance that Nick does, after talking to him one becomes aware of his really rich personality."

"Yes," said Betsy, "Dave is intellectually alert, and I most like his capacity to be serious-minded as well as sprightly." Betsy was pleased to say, "I've invited Dave to come out and

play some of his favorite pieces on the piano and he said that
some evening he would come and do that."

Two nights later, Dave paid the call he had promised. For
over an hour, he sat at the piano and played song after song
that Betsy requested. Finally, they sat before the wood fire
and talked. Dave asked Betsy if she thought Uncle John
might be impressed by a booklet he was writing about local
industries.

"Yes, I should think so." She told of the interest Uncle John
showed last spring in an article in the *Farm Journal* about
the spraying of apple trees, the writer of which was a man
he knew who lived in Waynesboro and worked in the Mont
Alto orchards. "Uncle John was so favorably impressed that
he talked of the writer as if he were an important person.
Your booklet might make a very favorable impression on
Uncle John."

"Have you been making much progress in your writing,
Dave?"

"I've become so engrossed in the art of writing that instead of studying law, I get up early each morning and practice writing. It is a difficult study and I must constantly discipline myself to keep at it, but if I ever succeed I will feel
very much like Joseph in Egypt when he said, 'Thou hast
made me fruitful in the land of my affliction.' "

"Dave, I don't want to be too personal, but I can't help
wondering what you mean by your reference to 'affliction.' "

Dave hesitated a long moment, "Well, for reasons I'd
rather not go into, I feel uncomfortable about having Nick
Mellers as a business partner. I hope to be able to buy his
interest in the shop very soon."

"Yes, I hope you can, too," Betsy said sympathetically.

At first, she was puzzled by Dave's description of his
"affliction." It had not been very long ago that Dave had described how helpful Nick had been to him in modernizing
the shop and now, for some reason, he felt they could no
longer work together.

The problems between Dave and Nick had begun at prep school where Dave excelled over Nick in sports. After Dave won the hundred yard dash and was assigned to the relay team, Nick's pride was hurt and for some time he had acted like a spoiled boy who could not have his way.

Nick's attitude toward Dave became evident to Betsy one evening at a dinner party given by the Nilsens. Dave and Nick were among the young people who were invited. The topic of conversation at dinner was the unique prosperity of Waynesboro. Every one had suggestions to which they attributed the town's financial success. Betsy suggested it was due to the thriftiness of the people of the "plain" churches such as Mennonites, River Brethren, and the Dunkers.

Dave cited the example of Abram Fischer. "He grew up on a farm on the outskirts of town, wore the plain garb, attended meeting all his life and lived apart from the world on the farm where he experimented with and invented a traction engine which he built in his shop in town. Later he added a threshing machine. The employees were skilled, owned stock in the company and took pride in its success."

"I wonder," Hans remarked, "if their money turned out to be a blessing or a blight."

Dave seemed sure that some were blessed by it, but not all. He added, "No doubt the creative interests of the founders have been marred whenever people became engrossed with gaining great wealth."

"How have you cultivated creative interests at the printery, Dave?" Karin asked.

He smiled and answered, "I suppose my efforts to be creative have consisted chiefly in keeping my heart free from feelings of ill will towards others when things didn't go right. I take seriously the passage in the New Testament, 1 John 3:14, which says 'He who does not love abides in death.' I believe love is genuinely creative."

"I wonder," Hans suggested, "if the practice of good will

might not be the best way to solve the difficulties between management and labor."

Nick's business-like mind had listened to talk about creative interests and love long enough. He burst out and said, "The managers of Waynesboro shops are bullheaded and downright stupid in business dealings."

"I wasn't aware that they'd been so stupid," Dave argued. "They were efficient enough to keep the shops operating even during the severe depression in the 1890's when many firms elsewhere had closed down."

Nick's face became red and he looked at Dave with contempt because he had disagreed with him and given such a clever reply. He would have continued the argument, but Betsy intervened in a joking way saying, "You can fight this out to the bitter end at the printery, but in the meantime, let's all go to the music room to hear the new duet Karin and Hans are going to play for us."

The argument had given Betsy an insight into Nick's character and she understood how difficult it must have been for Dave to be in partnership with him.

During the summer months Betsy spent much of her time at Uncle John's helping Aunt Salina with the gardening and canning. She went to Woodwinds frequently and at times visited at Dave's to practice on the piano, too.

One morning after family worship and breakfast at Uncle John's, Amos said he would like to talk with Betsy, so they went out for a little walk. Betsy began by commending Amos for his great interest in the farm work, but added, "Amos, are you interested in more schooling after high school?"

"No," he said," I want to learn farming from A to Z from Uncle John. What I wanted to ask, Betsy, is what would you think if I were to join the Old Order Church.

"Oh, Amos, that would be truly wonderful!" she beamed. "Why Amos, you would be following in the family ways. I've been worried that perhaps you would decide not to join because I hadn't."

"Ach, Betsy," he said with a serious expression, "you must never have a bad conscience about that. I remember you saying to Papa that you didn't have a call to become an Old Order, and you know, I've thought a good deal about that even though I didn't know then what it meant. I wouldn't be surprised but that I do have something like a call to join. Betsy, I want to tell you myself and not have you hear it from anybody else, but I like Mary Harshberger very much and she and I might join the church at the same time."

"Good, Amos! I'm with you one hundred percent! Mary certainly was a sweet little girl when I used to see her, and she's in your class in high school, isn't she?"

"Oh, and bright as a beam of sunshine," he said with a chuckle. "But you know, she likes the Old Order so much, she says she couldn't be contented in any other church."

"Amos, you cannot imagine how greatly this pleases me to realize that you will be carrying on the family tradition."

Early in August Betsy received an invitation from Dave to attend the thirty-fifth anniversary of his printery, established by his great grandfather O'Lear. Mrs. O'Lear had invited some friends into their home, a lithographer from the Philadelphia School of Design was going to read a paper and Dave would play a solo or two. Betsy was, of course, eager to attend and mentioned it to Uncle John, but when he objected rather vehemently, she said she would respect his views and would not attend.

But during the hours of the anniversary party Betsy indulged in imagining the scene. She imagined she could hear Dave playing the piano and guessed the compositions he selected. All that evening Betsy pictured Dave's home and the forty guests enjoying the party; and when she smiled to herself that she was actually thinking so constantly of Dave, she realized that she had become unusually fond of him, and she smiled to realize that Uncle John had caused her unusual preoccupation with Dave this evening!

Of course, Uncle John's choice for Betsy was still Paul

Honstein. He would often drop by for a call on Betsy and usually stayed to enjoy a meal with the family. Uncle John commented to Aunt Salina that Paul and Betsy certainly had lots to talk about.

The Saturday after Dave's party, Paul came by in the afternoon. He handed Betsy a bag of doughnuts his mother made for her. When they sat out on the porch together he talked to her about the Old Order Church and asked why she didn't join.

"Paul, although I have great respect for the Old Order, I just don't feel at home there. I was pleased, though, when I heard that Amos planned to join." Paul's eyes lost all their luster as she talked. Although he cheered up during the evening he seemed moody again when it was time for him to go.

On Sunday morning Betsy was present at family worship which Uncle John held regularly every morning in the sitting room before breakfast. When his three sons and three daughters were children, it was understood they were to be dressed and present when their father was ready. The oldest son was rearing his family on a farm nearby; he had recently been elected a preacher by the Old Order congregation, which gave great satisfaction to his father, who many years ago had been advanced to the eldership. The two oldest daughters were married and lived on farms near Chambersburg, and their children had early united with the church and donned the plain garb. Ann was the youngest of Uncle John's children and although she always attended service with her parents, she still hadn't joined the church.

Uncle John's "congregation" for this morning's worship consisted of Aunt Salina, Ann, and Betsy, and her brothers. They sang a hymn, beginning, "Lord, in the morning Thou shalt hear My voice ascending high," and then Uncle John read the first psalm and the seventh chapter of the gospel of Luke. He talked about how the strong faith of the Roman centurion was especially pleasing to the Lord. As Betsy listened to these comments she noticed Aunt Salina's uneasiness, and learned afterwards that she feared she hadn't pulled the skillet back far enough on the kitchen range and the mush would be burned. As she said afterwards to Betsy, "I got afraid Pop would forget himself and keep on talking about the Roman centurion!" As her mush was burned she set about immediately to fry freshly cut slices, and after a time they had an enjoyable breakfast.

Betsy drove with the family to the Rising Spring Church near Chambersburg and felt pride once more in the stately dignity of the colonial stone church. Everybody gave Betsy a hearty welcome as she walked with the others to the entrance of the meetinghouse, and she felt it was pleasant to be back in the familiar surroundings of her childhood. Inside the church she sat as usual on the rear seat, on the right-hand side, with Cousin Ann. She could remember how happy she felt when she was first permitted to sit with the girls on the last row.

After the first hymn, which an elder "lined" before each verse was sung, Betsy became aware after a very long prayer by another of the elders of the change that had come over her feeling and thinking about the Old Order. She thought of the beautiful liturgical service of the Lutheran Church to which she had responded when attending a service with Hans and Karin. As she listened to three sermons she felt there was a good deal of severity in the views set forth by the elders. She smiled to herself in remembering how earlier generations had lamented that their times were so bad, and still this generation had the idea that these times were the worst.

She thought to herself, *Perhaps I've become too worldly minded. Ach, no,* she told herself, *I'm not as worldly-minded as when I was in high school, but the elders now are certainly upset about the young people.*

Betsy was pleased to see Uncle John get up to preach the last sermon, and he was so much like her father and Uncle Abe, for in his brief sermon he explained how each one can by faith experience the peace that only Christ can give, which the world cannot give. There was no place in his sermon for scolding. Betsy thought of dear Aunt Salina so completely happy in the Old Order Church and understood it fulfilled helpfully a spiritual need for those within the fold. She was thankful that Amos was going to become an Old Order.

After a bountiful dinner Betsy waited until Uncle John had settled comfortably in his rocking chair on the porch. Then she went out and sat on the top step and looked up into his face as she told him that Johnny had talked to her and revealed he would like to go to college after graduating from high school next spring.

Uncle John looked offended and blurted out, "Ach, no, Betsy, I tell you I don't like you to do this to me!"

"Uncle John, I'm only trying to help my brothers who do express interest and want to make something of themselves. Johnny has become interested in literature and he thinks he would like to become a teacher. This, Uncle John, is a compelling interest which I cannot ignore, and I am very sorry that it makes you so unhappy." Uncle John remained quiet for a little while. Then he lamented, "There's not much chance that Johnny will ever become Old Order if he goes away to college." This cheerless mood shortly gave way to an amiable mood as he smiled and asked, "Tell me, Betsy, you like Paul pretty good, don't you?"

"Why, yes, Uncle John, Paul and I get along very well."

"Now tell me, Betsy, wouldn't you like to be his wife?"

"Uncle John, I can think well of Paul as a friend but not as a husband. I can tell you that I pray every day for guidance about being in love, as I certainly want to be sure my marriage will be 'in the Lord' as the Apostle Paul expressed it. Frankly, I don't feel I could ever love Paul, though I have respect for him as a person. But the fact is I am beginning to feel that I love Dave, just as you warned me! He has been a most helpful friend and I think he would be the right man for my husband. I am not engaged to him, and I will never marry him without your complete approval, but that is how I feel and I am trusting the Lord for guidance."

Uncle John's face became red as he stood up, "Betsy, I will never approve of Dave, and you might as well recognize that fact! I can't see what's gotten into you—a girl that shows at times good common sense and at other times you act like a wild person with no training at all! I simply can't understand you refusing to accept Paul for your husband and caring for that O'Lear boy."

"Uncle John, I wish you would believe me when I tell you I'm not trying to have my own way so much as I'm really trying to learn what is God's will for me. All I ask of you is that you pray I might have for a husband the man the Lord approves of."

"I can't tell you how disappointed I am in you," he said as he strode into the house, leaving Betsy on the porch alone.

A week later word came from Aunt Mattie that Uncle Abe had had a stroke. Betsy offered to go down and help because Aunt Mattie didn't approve of taking Abe to the hospital. She solved the problem of nursing by having two of her daughters come, and she was especially pleased with Betsy for offering to take her turn at nursing.

Each day after Betsy served for eight hours as a nurse, she used her free time to do what chores were needed; towards the end of the week when Uncle Abe began to show signs of recognition and could speak a few words, she read to him from the Bible and his eyes showed real appreciation. When Aunt Mattie saw how helpful and efficient Betsy was in managing the details of the sick room, and in being kind to Uncle Abe, she couldn't praise her enough. She remarked that after Betsy's visit in their home over last Christmas when Betsy had a long talk with Uncle Abe about her various interests, Uncle Abe said that Betsy was a most unusual person and ought to be appreciated, and he was going to pray for God's blessing and guidance in her life. When Betsy's week was up and she was returning to Uncle John's, Aunt Mattie thanked her again and again, but first she wanted Betsy to explain to her daughter, Thelma, who had come to do the nursing, all that was involved in taking care of the patient.

Unfortunately, Thelma had the same disposition as her mother and the two quarreled frequently. Within a few days there was unbearable friction between the two, and one afternoon not more than a week after Betsy had gone, Aunt Mattie scolded Thelma so severely in the sick room that Uncle Abe had a second stroke and died before evening.

Aunt Mattie was dazed! She hardly knew what she was doing! She took upon herself all the blame for her husband's death and seemed overwhelmed with remorse. When Betsy came for the funeral, Aunt Mattie kissed her and took her by the arm as they walked into the parlor to see the body of Uncle Abe. There Aunt Mattie broke down and sobbed that she was responsible for his death and had suffered so greatly that she had resolved on her knees in prayer that she would never again permit herself to lose her temper. At the close of the funeral when only the relatives remained, Aunt Mattie said in the presence of Uncle John and the others that Uncle Abe said one day "the family ought to face the fact that Betsy isn't going to become Old Order and we ought to do whatever we can to help her have a good life," and he added that in his judgment "she could have a good life with Dave better than with anyone else."

Uncle John looked deeply solemn as he said, "Everybody knows Brother Abe was a man of wisdom who manifested the love of God." They returned home to Pennsylvania, leaving Aunt Mattie in her sorrow.

15

Yule at Woodwinds

DAVE RECEIVED AN INVITATION from the Nilsens to be their guest in their celebration of Yule. Elaborate preparations were made for the holiday. First Karin gave the house a thorough cleaning following Norwegian custom, then days were devoted to baking cakes and cookies. She baked fourteen different cakes, a special one for each day.

The Sunday before Christmas, the Nilsen's son, Rolfe, arrived from Minnesota with his wife and sons. No one could be around Hans without catching some of his youthful enthusiasm for Christmas. Each day when he came home he had a special task planned. To help him he had his two flaxen-haired grandsons. Little Hans was nine and Erik was five. They put up decorations and searched the woods for just the right tree. Little Hans and Erik ran ahead and found a large yellow pine. Their grandfather cut it down, then they carried it home. It soon filled the whole house with its fresh fragrance. The tree was placed in the sun parlor and of course, everyone present took part in the fun of trimming it with handmade ornaments and colored paper chains.

The sun parlor was decorated in such a way that one could easily forget that he was in Pennsylvania and imagine himself in a charming home in Norway. On the walls were large pictures of the Nilsen's favorite Norwegian scenes. One whole wall was covered with a large handwoven tapestry. A ledge above the windows was filled with carved wooden plates and wrought-iron candlesticks. In the box with the Christmas ornaments, Little Hans and Erik found the carved wooden figures of boys and girls dressed to go skiing. With help from their grandfather they placed the figures on the mantelpiece where they had been every Christmas since Karin was a little girl in Norway.

By Thursday, the day before Christmas, Thor and his wife and two daughters arrived from their home in Michigan, and they all exclaimed there was certainly no place for spending Christmas like Grandfather's home!

Dave was the last of the guests to arrive late Thursday afternoon. From the moment he got out of his buggy he seemed like a ten-year-old as he exclaimed, "Merry Christmas to all, Merry Christmas to all!" until he reached the door, where Betsy and everybody welcomed him as if he were one of the family.

The warm weather that week prevented snow, but an exciting Christmas spirit prevailed indoors. The dinner that Christmas Eve brought refreshment and good cheer. Although the children clamored to be allowed to carry the bowl of porridge to the porch of the shed for the Julesvenn, that privilege was granted to Kristin, the pretty eight-year-old daughter of Thor, who explained to Dave about the Julesvenn. Kristin had been carrying the bowl of porridge outdoors for them ever since she was four years old. Dave was glad for Betsy's hint to bring gifts for each of the children. He thought he had never seen a happier child than Kristin.

After dinner everyone joined in singing Norwegian carols and folk songs, with Karin at the piano, until it was time for the children to go to bed and the adults left for the Christmas Eve service at the Lutheran church.

Early Friday morning the children eagerly rushed to empty the stockings hanging at the fireplace. Each child was thrilled with the toys and candy they found. After breakfast everyone assembled at the Christmas tree, and Karin, Betsy, and Hans played instrumental trios of Norwegian Christmas songs, followed by a period of worship when Hans read from the gospel of Luke about Mary and the Babe. Then he offered prayer as he had been doing on Christmas morning for many years. The rest of the morning was filled with music and singing while the children played with their new toys.

Shortly after noon guests began arriving for the Christmas dinner, called Julemiddag, which was served in the large dining room at one-thirty to twenty guests, eight in addition to the family. During the afternoon while the younger children took naps, some of the adults went on walks up the slope but for the most part they seemed to like to be in the music room. Betsy and Dave took a walk up the slope, where Dave took pictures of the scenery but he always wanted to include Betsy, insisting that she enhanced the beauty of the scene. He thought Betsy looked especially lovely in a very becoming dress—a red print on an ivory ground, with a full skirt, and declared that the chic Norwegian sweater she put on for their walk added to her beauty.

"This is so much nicer than last Christmas, Betsy. You were at your Aunt Mattie's and I was at home thinking of how I missed you. That was when I realized I had begun to love you, and now I love you more than ever before. Betsy, I don't want to ever spend another Christmas without you. Will you be my wife?"

There was a long pause. Tears welled up in Betsy's eyes as she tried so hard to say just what she felt. "Oh you know, Dave, how I feel, don't you? It's wonderful, so wonderful, to know we are really engaged to be married. I want to thank the Lord every day for your love.

"Very soon we'll have to drive out to Uncle John's and ask his approval of our engagement. I waited until I was twenty-one as I promised so I think he'll approve," she added.

The air had become much colder, so Betsy and Dave returned to the house. They announced their engagement to no one, but Betsy's happy glow and Dave's contentment suggested to everyone that they were in love. Dave and Betsy sang and played the piano with greater joy than ever before.

After the guests had departed, Betsy and Dave sat before a crackling wood fire with Karin and Hans, and she told them of her engagement to Dave. Hans stood up with youthful zest and said, "I feel like singing, 'Praise God from Whom All Blessings Flow'! I am pleased, Betsy, that you had the good sense to accept this young man's proposal. Congratulations, Dave, on winning a lovely girl." He became more serious, however, when he asked Betsy, "What about your Uncle John?"

"Dave and I are going to go to Uncle John and ask his approval."

"That's fine!" replied Hans. "I've come to have a sort of sneaking admiration for your Uncle John as a virile personality, despite his peculiarities, such as his naive insistence that a boy is shiftless if he shows any fondness for a good time! I don't like to indulge in gloomy predictions, but judging from what Uncle John thinks of Dave, I fear he may turn down Betsy's request for his approval. If he does, it would be wise for you to keep trying to win his consent and blessing. Many young people today would ignore Uncle John and get married regardless of what he thought, but since marriage is a blessed institution ordained by the Almighty, I think it would be well to gain your uncle's approval. Try for a year or maybe two and if by that time he still objects, marry without his consent."

"I agree with you completely, Hans, and that's just what we intend to do," Dave assured him. "In the meantime, Betsy and I will have an opportunity to select some nice old house in the country near Waynesboro and set about remodeling it."

Karin mentioned, "I think I'll heed an impulse I've had and write a letter to your Uncle John and tell him my opinion of Dave. It may be of some help."

Hans and Karin became busy preparing for more guests who were coming for coffee in the evening, and Dave and Betsy talked as they sat before the fire. "Betsy," he began, "I'm glad you encouraged me to write the sketch of Waynesboro's industries. I enjoyed doing the research and reading all the historical sketches published by the various firms. It even gave me the opportunity to meet people who had known some of the founders. You'll be interested to know that I called on Uncle John to inquire about the founder of the Fischer Company whom he had known when he was a boy. He told me some things that had never before been recorded. Why, he got so interested in telling me what he knew about Abram Fischer that he seemed to forget his prejudice against me and was more genial that I have ever seen him. And he didn't once bring up about my being a spender and riding on that pony! The sketch is all finished now and is being printed. I've titled it *The Romance of Waynesboro Industries*."

"This was something that really needed to be written to give people pride in the community. I hope the Old Order people will appreciate it. I know it will change Uncle John's attitude toward you better than anything else," Betsy exclaimed proudly.

"A few weeks ago, I wrote to the twins," Dave added. "I explained their father's attitude and the difficulty it caused us and they said they would write to Uncle John and explain that I was not responsible for their refusal to join the Old Order."

"Oh, Dave, that's wonderful. I want so much for Uncle John to be persuaded to like you. I promised not to marry without his consent and I know it would break his heart if I went against my word. He may be stubborn, but I love him and I hope he can be persuaded."

"Yes, by all means, Betsy, I can see that you are right about it, and I shall keep at it until I succeed." After a few moments of silence as he watched the burning logs, Dave smiled and commented, "You know, sometimes it puzzles me how your aunts and uncles could be so interesting even though they've never had much formal training."

Betsy's eyes flashed, and her voice was firm, as she declared, "They're interesting because they are real people with unique personalities. Oh, Dave, please don't permit yourself ever to think that you have to be highly educated to be an interesting or important person. Think of Aunt Salina; the only book she knows is the Bible but she's interesting because of her appreciation of beauty. The apostles Jesus chose were interesting people with a capacity for being spiritual, though according to the snobbish Pharisees they were 'unlearned and ignorant men.' If only my Uncle John could be delivered from his prejudices he would be a really interesting person."

"Oh, to be sure, Betsy, you win this argument absolutely!" laughed Dave, and he admitted he made that remark just to see what Betsy would say, and he was thankful that he agreed with her absolutely.

Later in the evening a group of friends came and everyone joined in singing Christmas carols again. It seemed that visitors to the Nilsens always looked forward to music and singing, so guests were habitually entertained in the music room.

When the other guests had gone and it was time for Dave to leave, Betsy walked him to the shed and thrilled him by quoting the opening lines of one of Shakespeare's sonnets,

> How like a winter hath my absence been
> From thee, . . .
> What freezings have I felt, what dark days seen!

Dave felt it must be true of her as she quoted the lines. He was unable to quote an appropriate verse in return because he was speechless with happiness as he held her hands tightly and looked into her eyes.

Betsy could not keep silent in her joy. She kept recalling line after line that she had memorized that reminded her of

Dave and her love for him. She remembered how Natásha described to her brother the pleasure she felt from her engagement to Prince Andrew, and she quoted aloud, " 'I feel at peace and settled. I know that no better man than he exists, and I am calm and contented now.' " Then she thought of the words of Jane Eyre expressed after ten years of her marriage to Edward Rochester, so she added, " 'I hold myself supremely blest—blest beyond with language can express.' "

"Oh, and I thank God that I've been blessed with you, Betsy!" exclaimed Dave as he kissed her good night.

On Saturday morning Betsy hitched up her team and left Woodwinds early, rejoicing in the glory of the new day, so fresh and invigorating, after it had snowed during the night. She quoted several passages to herself from Shakespeare about the dawn as she rode along. The weather was sharp and clear and cold. She met Dave at his office and he declared there was no question now about his succeeding with his present work. As he reflected on the printery he could see possibilities and attractions he had never thought of before, and he reminded her that his sketch of *The Romance of Wallaceburg Industries* which she inspired him to write was now being printed. Betsy then drove out to Uncle John's. She had phoned Mrs. O'Lear and asked her to tell Uncle John that she had to see him about an important matter.

Aunt Salina, Ann, and the boys gave Betsy a hearty welcome. Shortly thereafter Uncle John came in from the barn and said he was ready to talk to her. His eyes looked sullen and Betsy feared that perhaps she had chosen the wrong time to come, but she remembered Dave and was anxious to tell everyone the news. While Aunt Salina and cousin Ann prepared the noon meal, Betsy and Uncle John went into the sitting room.

As soon as they were alone, Betsy told Uncle John she had become engaged to Dave and came out to ask for his approval. Uncle John stood up and looked at her with a dull, resentful expression. He took off his glasses and began pulling at his beard, but he was otherwise calm and forceful, and talked to Betsy as he might to a group of elders. "If you had joined the Old Order when your pop wanted you to, you would know for certain what I would say about Dave. But I must say I'm shocked at you asking me like this. You know already what I think of him, and I warned you often enough that I didn't want to hear any talk about you marrying him! If your Uncle Abe was still living and was your guardian, he would no doubt approve of Dave. Down at his house after the funeral, I did think well of his views, but since then I've had enough reason for doubts. I heard Nick Mellers is getting out of the printery, and when that happens, then Dave's finished; that's the penalty for not sticking to his work with all his might."

Betsy felt a shudder pass through her as she listened. His onslaught had somehow overawed her and she couldn't marshal her argument as she had planned, but she tried to reason, and thought of a point, "You speak of Nick Mellers' getting out of the printery as if that's bad for Dave, but do you realize Nick is getting out because Dave has bought out his share and will not tolerate him in the firm any longer?"

Uncle John's eyes opened wide, and he was silent for a moment, "No, I didn't know that! Why, that does mean something different fom what I was given to understand. Betsy, I have to keep in mind the O'Lears are my neighbors and I try to get along good with them but the fact is, the Lord provided parents and guardians to look after the welfare of children, and one must do his duty."

Betsy thought to herself she had never seen Uncle John at a greater disadvantage. His sullen look seemed so unnatural in one whom she had always thought of as a kind, sympathetic, understanding person, but now he seemed to be showing positive ill will. She suddenly realized that enumerating to herself Uncle John's shortcomings would accomplish nothing. "I have every confidence, Uncle John, that you are aiming to do only what you think is best for me. Would you do me a favor?"

"Well, it all depends on what it is," he replied grudgingly.

"I want you to go to your brother Zeke and ask if he ever heard of any negligence Dave has shown in attending to his work at the printery. When you speak of the penalty for not sticking to his work with all his might, please tell me where you learned that."

Betsy looked at Uncle John with such a penetrating look that he must have felt he couldn't afford to ignore her earnest plea, for he promised to do as she asked. "I might as well admit it was Nick who told me."

"Why, Uncle John, I must say I'm shocked that you, an upright man of God, you let a scamp and deceiver like Nick fill you with lies about other people whom Nick wants to get the better of."

Aunt Salina overheard most of the conversation between her husband and Betsy, and when she had a chance to talk to Betsy alone in the kitchen, she whispered, "I heard what you told Pop. Just put your trust in the Lord, dear,—it will work out all right in the end. We'll just have to be patient until Pop sees the light! And he will because he has a kind heart. Nick's been so cunning in talking to Pop of late and putting ideas into his head that they begin to develop and he doesn't know what to believe."

Betsy threw her arms around Aunt Salina and kissed her a half-dozen times to thank her, and wiped the tears from her eyes. At dinner the boys were so eager to talk to their sister that she chatted with them and laughed. Everyone was interested in hearing about the Christmas celebration at the Nilsens. Uncle John, though, had very little to say.

After helping Aunt Salina and Ann with the dishes, Betsy left for town and met Dave again at his office. The gloom in her eyes told the bad news even before she said a word. Dave remained cheerful. "I didn't expect a favorable verdict from

Uncle John right away! It'll be the most interesting assignment I've ever had to convince him I am worthy to be your husband."

Dave surprised Betsy by handing her a copy of his sketch of the industries of Waynesboro. She sat down and read it through, and was pleased beyond measure! "It's so interesting, so well done, and I'm sure Uncle John will be favorably impressed."

Dave and Betsy spent the remainder of the afternoon driving around the countryside looking at old houses which they might buy and fix up for their home. The last place they stopped was the old Yingling farmhouse that Dave had always liked. It was close to Altenwald, a hamlet of twenty-five families a few miles north of town. When they inspected it, Betsy agreed it had excellent possibilities. Dave rejoiced to say that the owner would sell.

Before going to Laura's for supper, Dave drove Betsy to the top of Burns's Hill to see the landscape covered with snow. They walked about from one vantage point to another admiring the wintry scene, now looking to the east towards Blue Mountain and now to the west across the twenty-five miles of the historic Cumberland Valley towards Tuscarora Mountain. Within a few minutes they stood in awe before the matchless beauty of the sunset, the valley blazed in orange fire which reflected on the snow. As the sun slowly dropped below the mountain, Betsy looked up into Dave's eyes and they kissed. As they watched the beauty of the sun slowly fade away, Betsy said, "I'm thankful to know there is nothing in life quite so wonderful as true love that does not fade away, but grows stronger with the years." They kissed again, then they drove back down Burns's Hill.

At Laura's home Dave played with six-year-old Sidney, Jr. while Betsy told her sister of the engagement. She was pleased but cautioned Betsy not to become too impatient and upset with Uncle John's stubbornness.

After dinner, Dave read his sketch about Waynesboro industries to Laura and Sidney. They heartily approved of his effort and suggested that if Uncle John could read it, his impression of Dave might be changed. Betsy decided to mail him a copy the next day.

16

Perseverance Pays

As Dave was returning home from work late Monday afternoon, he drove up John Butterbaugh's lane and walked to the chicken house where he saw that Uncle John was at work. Uncle John's clothes were white with lime as he came out to invite Dave to come to the house.

"I don't want to interrupt your work, Mr. Butterbaugh. We can talk right here. I've come to ask if you would be good enough to approve of my engagement to Betsy."

Uncle John looked sterner than usual. "I'll tell you plainly that there are certain reasons why I can't approve of you as a husband for Betsy. For one thing, you're too free with money just like your father was. He went and spent money on you when you should have been earning your own. Do you keep a record of all the money you spend?"

"Well, sir, I record any big sums I spend but not the smaller ones because in regard to any expenditure I've always asked myself if it was prudent to spend a certain amount or—"

Uncle John interrupted bluntly, "A thrifty man keeps a record of every penny."

"Well, sir, I hate a debt as much as anyone."

"Oh, really, well how careful were you to pay off your debt at the printery?"

"The printery lost a good deal of business when all the

other shops in town slowed down so I wasn't able to pay off my debt as quickly as I had hoped to. I'm hopeful that business will improve again soon."

"Such high hopes make a pretty flimsy foundation for good finances. Just how much are you spending on yourself?" he asked squinting his eyes at him.

"I spend very little on myself. You know I don't smoke or drink."

Uncle John blurted out, "But how much are you spending on foolishness like the piano?"

When Dave explained he felt warranted in spending money on something that would do his soul good, Uncle John was exasperated, "How can you spend money on such stuff when you're in debt? You don't seem to realize what a dreadful thing it is to have such a debt hanging over you still."

Dave was stunned to realize that Uncle John had heard of his new piano. He wondered if he should continue the conversation. But Uncle John was far from finished.

"There's another count of long standing I have against you, Dave O'Lear, and I cannot overlook it. My twin sons would be members of the Old Order today if you hadn't turned them against it."

"We've discussed this before, Mr. Butterbaugh. There's nothing I can do if you won't believe my explanation."

"Yes," Uncle John replied, "I got letters from the twins saying you weren't to blame for them turning against their family church, but how could I accept that? If there had been no Dave O'Lear around when the twins was growing up and playing with you, those boys would have joined the Old Order. I'm going to be firm in standing by what I know to be true and right, so I want you to realize I cannot approve of you as a husband for Betsy."

"Well, Mr. Butterbaugh, I'll be going. I can see your mind is made up. I wish you would not be too assured about what you say you know is true and right. Please pray about it."

Uncle John looked at him and said, "Well, yes!"

Dave hurried out to see Betsy within an hour of his fruitless call on Uncle John, hoping that the two of them could devise other ways of dealing with him, but she reiterated the dependence she put on Dave's sketch, and said they would have to bide their time.

The next day, Tuesday, after the morning chores were done, Uncle John sat in the kitchen looking over the mail he had just brought from town. He held in his hand a letter from Mrs. Nilsen, held it out, looking at it curiously as if here was something special! Then he read it. She wrote of Betsy's interest in Dave. She assumed that Mr. Butterbaugh would like to learn how Dave impressed both her and her husband. She said that of all the young men she had become acquainted with, Dave impressed her as having the most pleasing disposition and he was certainly a man of character, and had impressed her husband as having an understanding of sound principles of finance and of business matters in general. Uncle John read this letter three times, remembering the fine impression he had received when he called at the Nilsen home.

The next envelope he opened contained Dave's booklet. At the end of two hours he had finished its more than thirty pages, and muttered to himself, "Could be I was too hard on him! Abe always defended him! I'll read this over again." He must have read the passages a half-dozen times where Dave praised the Old Order leaders for their substantial contribution to the industrial development in town, and mentioned their solidity of character and personal integrity, though some were too easily prejudiced. Uncle John rocked slowly in his chair, then sat motionless. "Why, can it be I have been so badly mistaken about Dave?" he asked himself. "Salina," he called, "Come here. I think I've been wrong about Dave. I should have listened to you and Betsy instead of Nick Mellers, who's been downright deceptive. I'm going down to see Mattie about this."

After John had gone, Salina hurried over to Dave's home and asked his mother to phone Betsy to tell her that "Pop be-

gins to see the light! And be sure to tell Betsy to thank Mrs.
Nilsen for such a wonderful letter."

When Betsy heard the news, she phoned Dave immediately and told him of her plans to go to Uncle John's the very
next afternoon. Dave was pleased at the good word but he
had just made an appointment in Harrisburg which he hoped
would produce some business for the printery. He was sorry,
but Betsy would have to go to Uncle John's alone.

Down at Aunt Mattie's John read to her the letter from Mrs.
Nilsen and a portion of Dave's sketch which he praised be-
yond measure; in fact, he thought it was "truly remarkable."
"After reading this, my objections to Dave seemed to vanish."

Mattie looked satisfied as she repeated what Abe had said,
and Uncle John admitted that Abe had been right.

"I hate to confess this, Mattie, but it's the sad truth that I
listened to what Nick Mellers kept telling me about Dave
and it was all lies. I tell you that young man Nick is too
clever for his own good. Why, he can be so convincing he
could almost make black seem to be white."

Betsy reached the Shady Gap farm shortly after the close
of school on Wednesday afternoon and was encouraged to
see that Uncle John's eyes had a kindly twinkle instead of the
sullen expression of her visit on Saturday. He seemed especially interested as Betsy told of the prospects Dave had
for a big order from Harrisburg and of his going there that
afternoon.

"You're not talking about Dave?" Uncle John's eyes were
smiling, "You mean," he said as he looked intently at her,
"he's going to tend business while you're in town and miss
being with you? That sounds odd after what I've heard about
him! Well, Betsy, I told Aunt Salina that she was right about
Dave and I was wrong. That little book of his about the
shops in town opened my eyes. It seemed to me it showed the
writer of it is a person to be admired because he has a gen-
erous, appreciative soul. Then, too, I did what you asked
me to do; I asked Zeke what he knew about Dave at his shop

and Zeke heard from one of the men who works for Dave that he tends to his work carefully every day. And what I said about the penalty for not sticking to his work, why that was what Nick was telling me at Zeke's store, to deceive me about Dave and his printery! So I've had my eyes opened about him, I'm thankful to say. But I'm afraid to give my full approval because Dave will likely do better if there's someone like me to hold him at arm's length and be critical. I think we'd better withdraw the agreement that you're not to get married without my approval."

"No, indeed!" said Betsy sternly, "Dave and I will not be married until we receive your full approval."

"Ach, now, Betsy, you're being stubborn again!" he said with a twinkle in his eyes.

"Now, John you know very well you approve of Dave as a husband for Betsy," said Aunt Salina, who had failed to see the twinkle.

"Yes, Salina, but I can't help but think it might be better for Dave's own good financially if someone kept a stern watch over him. Of course, Betsy, I approve of you and him getting married. I think that after a few years if Dave shows he has gotten rid of his debts and knows how to support a wife, why, then your Aunt Salina and I will make you a present, and of course, you should understand that you will now receive your full share of your pop's estate."

Betsy thanked him and asked if he realized that Dave thought highly of him. "One day he remarked that Uncle John's constant emphasis on being thrifty and keeping out of debt had made an impression on him and consequently he was no longer going to spend money as freely as before."

Betsy thanked him for agreeing to provide for her out of her father's estate. "Now I'll be able to provide for Jakie and Johnny all through college." When she had Aunt Salina by herself she gave her a special hug and kisses for her message by phone. "When the boys come home, be sure to tell them that Dave and I are engaged, because they've wanted it to happen for a long time."

Dave had not yet returned from Harrisburg when Betsy reached his office, so she wrote him a note telling what Uncle John had said, and added that she hoped he could come out to Woodwinds or else phone.

After making a brief call on her sister Laura she drove down to call on Aunt Mattie before returning to Woodwinds. She found her aunt in the kitchen peeling potatoes for her supper.

"Well, what in the world can be wrong to bring you here?"

"Oh no, Aunt Mattie," Betsy said cheerily, "I just drove down to tell you that Uncle John has agreed for me to get married to Dave."

Aunt Mattie's expression cleared when she saw Betsy's shining eyes, "Well, Betsy," she said with a smile, "you certainly deserve a good man! Your Uncle Abe knew all along that Dave would turn out all right. Your Uncle John came down to see me the other day and asked my advice. I told him how much Uncle Abe respected Dave without even reading his sketch about the shops in town. We agreed that Dave would be a fine husband for you, especially now after this booklet of his. Why, you should have heard your Uncle John go on about Dave for what he wrote about the shops!"

"I want to do the right thing about Paul, Aunt Mattie. He's a fine person and I wouldn't want to hurt him. I plan to write him a letter to inform him of my engagement to Dave and thank him for his friendship."

"Yes, Betsy, that would be the kind thing to do, but don't you fret about Paul. His mother tells me Sally Bringmann, who you know is a sister, is so eager for Paul to like her. She would make him a wonderful wife."

"That would be a good match," Betsy said, much relieved.

As Betsy drove up to Waynesboro and out to Woodwinds, she tried to imagine how Dave would react to her note. She was enchanted, her heart fluttering with love. *It will be such a thrill just to talk to him this evening on the phone,* she thought. She occupied her mind during the rest of the drive by trying to visualize what their home in the country would be like. It would be such a wonderful place to raise their children. She thanked God again for His many blessings in her life.

Then she imagined how fine it would be to be baptized by her Uncle Henry in Huntingdon and join the Dunker church in town as she and Dave had planned. For the first time she would be able to work in the church and eventually they could send their children to Sunday school there.

As Betsy came up the drive at Woodwinds, she could hear someone playing her and Dave's favorite music, Mozart's Piano Concerto in C Major. As she walked up the path, she caught a glimpse of Dave in the music room. Running into the house as fast as she could, she threw her arms around his neck, exclaiming excitedly, "Uncle John realized he was wrong; he likes you; he said we can get married!"

Dave was thrilled at the good news. He had brought some, too, for his trip to Harrisburg had produced a large order for the print shop.

"Oh, Dave, my mind is so filled with exciting thoughts of our wedding and our new home and the Lord's goodness to us that I just can't take it all in!"

"I know, Betsy. I feel the same way—happily confused. You know, if I ever collect my thoughts, I'd like to write a novel about the people of the Old Order—people like your parents and Aunt Mattie and Uncle John. And my very next book would be about my happy life with my wife, Betsy."

"But you should write it all in one book," Betsy corrected lovingly. "In spite of our differences and misunderstandings, we all belong to the Lord of glory and live to praise Him in our daily life."